"I do   dn't remain friends when you go back to L.A.," Rachel said.

"Because I don't feel like your friend." His words came out on a sigh and he leaned his forehead against hers. "Not at all." After a moment he took her hand and pulled her to her feet.

Rachel let out her breath. "I like you, Jay." She whispered the words. "So much."

Jay straightened and his eyes met hers, the depths of emotion taking her breath away. "With a face like mine, I can't imagine why."

Rachel realized that she no longer saw Jay Nordstrom, the popular newscaster who'd once made the cover of a magazine, but a man who, in only a few short weeks, had found a place in her heart.

Impulsively Rachel leaned forward and gently kissed his battered cheek. "Any woman would be lucky to have you."

CYNTHIA RUTLEDGE

loves writing romance because a happy ending is guaranteed! Writing for Steeple Hill allows her to combine her faith in God with her love of romance. When she's not writing romance or working full-time as health network consultant for a large insurance company, Cynthia likes to take long walks with her husband, chat on the phone with her daughter and attend theater productions with her friends.

For Love's Sake is Cynthia's eleventh book for Steeple Hill Love Inspired®. Cynthia loves to hear from readers and encourages you to visit her Web site at www.cynthiarutledge.com.

FOR LOVE'S SAKE

CYNTHIA RUTLEDGE

Steeple
Hill®

Published by Steeple Hill Books™

STEEPLE HILL BOOKS

Steeple
Hill®

ISBN 0-373-87291-7

FOR LOVE'S SAKE

www.SteepleHill.com

Printed in U.S.A.

The LORD does not look at the things
man looks at. Man looks at the outward appearance,
but the LORD looks at the heart.

—*1 Samuel* 16:7

To Carolyn Jean Brown, who suggested I bring Rachel and Jay together in a book of their own. Until your letter, I hadn't even considered that the two secondary characters from *Redeeming Claire* would be a good match. But, Carolyn, you were right! Thanks for the suggestion and for letting Rachel finally find the happiness she deserved.

Chapter One

"Don't even think about it." Jay Nordstrom's hard unyielding voice shot across the room, breaking the silence that had permeated the old farmhouse all morning.

Rachel Tanner's hand paused in midair and her lips tipped upward in satisfaction. Finally she'd gotten a reaction. Until now Jay had ignored her, pretending to be reading even though the light in the living room was so dim it was a wonder he could see, much less read.

Taking a deep breath, Rachel reached forward and jerked open the heavy brocade draperies, letting the June sunlight bathe the room in light. She ignored Jay's cry of outrage and for a moment reveled in the feel of the warm sun against her face.

"It's much too beautiful a day to be holed up here in darkness," she said firmly.

"Shut them," he ordered. "Shut them now."

Rachel took a deep breath and counted to ten. Jay reminded her of her father when he used that tone of voice, and it wasn't a pleasant comparison. But she told herself that Jay had been through a lot in the past month. It was to be expected that he'd be a bit testy.

For now, she'd cut him some slack and hope that the sunlight would improve his mood. She turned from the window and met his glare with a bright smile.

Rachel couldn't say she really knew him. Though they'd grown up in the same small town, he'd been a couple years older and they'd run in different social circles. She'd been a bookworm, shy and studious, while he'd been an outgoing guy who never cracked a book. Despite that fact, he'd been a good student and everyone knew he'd make it big some day.

And he *had* made it big. After graduating with a degree in broadcasting from Drake University in Des Moines, Jay had headed west. He'd started his career at a small television station just outside San Francisco. But he hadn't stayed long. His rise up the newscasting ladder had been meteoric. It hadn't hurt that he was remarkably photogenic. Or that he'd garnered some great press of his own because of the modeling he'd done on the side to supplement his salary.

He returned to Millville only sporadically, usually on holidays. The last time Rachel had seen him was when he'd attended church with his family on Christmas Eve. Of course, he hadn't even looked her way when he'd walked past. But when he'd taken his seat at the end of the pew one row up and over, Rachel had definitely looked *him* over.

His mother volunteered at the school where Rachel taught and Twyla had regaled Rachel with stories of her successful, good-looking son for years. Rachel had seen him on TV, of course, but she'd been curious to see if the real man lived up to the image.

His hair was what she'd noticed first. It had glistened like spun gold in the light streaming through the clapboard church's stained-glass windows. Though she assessed him with a critical eye, after several minutes of careful scrutiny, Rachel was forced to admit that television hadn't done him justice. His boyishly handsome features had only improved with age. Without a doubt, the best-looking boy at Millville High had grown up to be a real hunk.

"Is that why you took this job?" Jay snapped, his tone harsh. "So that you could stare at the freak and then run home and tell all your friends the gory details?"

His words jerked Rachel from her reverie and she realized with horror that while her mind had wandered she'd been staring.

She stifled a groan. What a way to start off a new job. His mother had warned her that Jay was supersensitive about his altered appearance.

"I'm sorry." Rachel unconsciously reverted to the soft dulcet tones she used with her first graders during the school year. "I really wasn't staring. I was just thinking about the last time you were in Millville."

He shifted his gaze out the window. "I wasn't a freak then."

"And you're not a freak now." Though she wanted to be sympathetic, irritation rippled through Rachel. From what she knew of the car accident last month, Jay was lucky to be alive. He should be praising God his life had been spared, rather than wallowing in self-pity.

She thought of little Timmy who'd been in her

classroom last year. The boy suffered from a rare genetic disorder that caused pain and disfigurement. Still, Timmy came to school every day with a smile on his face. But then, Timmy hadn't once been handsome, either, she reminded herself. And he'd had years to adjust to his situation, not just a few weeks.

For the first time since she'd entered the room, Rachel really looked at Jay. A long red scar cut a swath across one cheek. The eye on that side was bloodshot and the skin surrounding it puffy and bruised. He might not be ready to be on the cover of *GQ*, but he didn't look as bad as his mother had indicated when Rachel had interviewed for the job as his temporary caretaker.

"So you have a scar across your cheek," she said. "And you look like you got socked in the eye. Big deal."

"What about this?" He gestured with his head to the cast that ran from his left foot up to his knee.

Rachel barely gave it, or the other cast on his right arm, a second glance.

"I was in a body cast for scoliosis when I was in junior high," Rachel said. "Don't expect any sympathy from me."

Jay's brows pulled together but instead of being

offended by her bluntness as she'd expected, his tightly controlled expression eased. "I thought nurses were supposed to be sympathetic."

He thought she was a nurse? The idea was laughable. The last time Rachel had tried to donate to the Red Cross, she'd fainted. The possibility of seeing any blood had been her only concern about accepting this position. But Twyla had repeatedly assured her there wouldn't be any open wounds.

"I don't know what your mother told you," she said. "But I'm a teacher, not a nurse."

He tilted his head and stared at her for a long moment. Finally, a dimple flashed in his left cheek, rippling the scar. "And what are you planning to teach me?"

Rachel laughed. "For starters, how about some manners?"

He shook his head, his gaze warming her skin. "We should start with something easier."

Rachel leaned back against the window and folded her arms across her chest. "What did you have in mind?"

"Kissing."

Her heart skipped a beat. Ever since she'd been in junior high, Rachel had fantasized about locking lips with Jay Nordstrom. "Kissing?"

Jay nodded and flashed a lazy smile. "I'd like some advanced lessons."

Rachel couldn't believe it. He'd oh-so-easily slipped into flirtatious mode. And she'd hazard a guess that the enticing smile he flashed usually got him whatever his heart desired.

"Sorry, Charlie." Rachel kept her tone deliberately light. "Not going to happen."

Kissing was one lesson Rachel wouldn't teach— not because of his injuries or because in this case the pupil would know more than the teacher, but because of Tom.

Jay's expression stilled and she could tell he wasn't accustomed to hearing the word no. "Because I'm ugly?"

Rachel rolled her eyes. "No."

"I don't believe you," he said flatly. "What other reason could there be?"

She couldn't believe his arrogance. He'd obviously never considered she might be dating someone. "I'm involved."

Surprise filled his eyes. "You're engaged?"

She shook her head. "No, but we are exclusive."

Jay heaved a sigh and leaned back in his chair. "Everyone in this town is either married, engaged or *involved.* It's…insane."

Rachel smiled. Insane wasn't the word she'd use—normal was the one that came to her mind.

"Even crazier, my mom told me Kim Krueger, my date for the senior prom, just had her third kid." Jay shook his head, a disbelieving look in his eye. "Tell me she made that up because she wants grandchildren."

"Kim's oldest was in my class last year," Rachel said, trying hard not to laugh.

"No kidding."

It seemed odd to be discussing old classmates with him but, when Rachel thought about it, what else did they really have in common? Jay hadn't lived in Millville since high school, and other than a brief stint in Chicago, Rachel hadn't lived anywhere else.

"Abby Zinsmaster has four," Rachel said. "Of course two are twins."

Jay grimaced. "Abby isn't old enough to have one child, let alone four."

"She's my age," Rachel reminded him. "Twenty-eight."

"I can't imagine being tied down like that at such a young age," Jay said. "Can you?"

Being married and having a family had been Rachel's dream since she'd been a preschooler clacking around in her mother's high heels, clutching a baby doll to her chest.

"Didn't I read you were dating someone fairly seriously?" Rachel asked, deliberately changing the subject. "Some model?"

"Lindsay Stark," Jay said in a flat tone.

"That's right." Lindsay was a provocative brunette rising to superstardom almost as fast as Jay had risen to become one of the most well-known newscasters in the country.

"And if you're asking if we're headed toward the altar, the answer is no." He absently rubbed his casted leg as if it ached. "I haven't seen Lindsay since shortly after the accident."

"Is she out of the country?" Though Rachel had no idea how the modeling world worked, she assumed there was a fair amount of travel involved.

"No." Jay leaned back in the chair and met her gaze. A weariness she hadn't noticed until now edged his eyes. "She's just busy."

Though his tone was offhand, the momentary flash of pain in his eyes confused her.

"What about you?" he asked. "Does your boyfriend live around here?"

Rachel nodded. "Actually he graduated with you. Tom Tidball?"

If she hadn't been staring directly into Jay's eyes she'd have missed the look of surprise. Though she understood the reaction, it still hurt. As the son of the former mayor and a star athlete in high school and college, Tom was Millville's "favorite son." He'd been part of the town's elite from the day he was born while, because of her father's explosive temper, she'd spent her life on the outside looking in.

Not anymore, she reminded herself. Being with Tom had opened those doors now to her, too.

"Tom and I were friends in high school," Jay said. "We played ball together."

They'd also partied together. But for Tom, all that was behind him. Now he ran his father's bank and a wild night on the town was dinner and a movie in Des Moines.

Jay's brows drew together. "I thought Tom married Karen Wheeler and moved to Kansas City."

"They split up two years ago. He moved back here last year." Rachel lifted her chin, uncomfortable with the direction of the conversation but not sure why.

"I know this makes me sound provincial," Jay said, "but it's weird to think that someone who graduated with me is already divorced."

"It *is* hard to believe," Rachel said with a rueful smile. She'd never planned to become involved with a divorced man, but Tom had swept her off her feet. "Unfortunately I see it every day. Probably half the kids in my classroom come from a single-parent household. I can only pray that my children will never have to split their time between mommy and daddy."

"That's why you need to make sure you marry the right guy."

"Exactly." Rachel gave Jay an approving glance. So many people thought that having a good marriage was just luck, but Rachel knew it was more than that; it was finding your soul mate, the person God intended you to be with for the rest of your life.

"Have you and Tom talked marriage?" he asked.

"Only in the most general of terms," Rachel said. "We want to take it slow. Make sure we're right for each other."

Curiosity flickered in Jay's eyes. "Sounds like you have some doubts?"

Rachel paused. She and Tom were working on their problems and she'd never been one to air her dirty laundry. "We have some issues to resolve."

"Do you two live together?"

"I don't believe in sex before marriage." Startled

by the unexpected question, Rachel responded immediately without bothering to censure her reply.

Jay's eyes widened as if she'd just announced she didn't believe in celebrating Christmas. "And Tom's okay with that?"

By the way he asked, Rachel knew Jay was having trouble reconciling the party guy he'd run around with as a teen to a man who could date a woman for three months without sleeping with her.

"Tom respects my decision," Rachel said.

Jay's lips curved up in a smile.

Irritation surged through Rachel at the look in his eye. "You think it's silly, don't you?"

"It doesn't make any sense." Jay absently rubbed the scar on his cheek with the side of his finger. "Today is all we have. Why not enjoy it?"

Rachel studied him for a long moment and wondered how he could have strayed so far from his roots and the Bible truths he'd been taught as a child. "You're used to such a different lifestyle. Why did you come back here to recuperate?"

It seemed a logical question. His father was busy in the fields, his mother was in Texas taking care of Jay's dying grandfather and his elderly great aunt could barely care for herself. "Wasn't there anyone in L.A. who could have helped you?"

Jay lifted a shoulder in a shrug. "I didn't want my friends to see me looking like a fr—"

He stopped at the warning look in her eye. "Like this."

Rachel thought how Dottie or Jocelyn or even Claire Karelli would be at her side in a heartbeat if she needed help. "But they're your friends."

"Friends who wouldn't hesitate to send their résumé to the station if they thought I might get the boot." Jay's tone was surprisingly philosophical.

Rachel started to protest, but immediately shut her mouth. Though she might still believe in the overall goodness of mankind, she was far from naive. Living eight months in a big city and working for a Fortune 500 company had opened her eyes to the sometimes evil ways of the world.

"I had friends like that when I lived in Chicago," Rachel said. "That's why I came back home."

"Seems like a drastic step," Jay drawled, his gaze fixed on her.

"You came back, too."

"Only on a temporary basis," he pointed out. "You're stuck here permanently."

"Not stuck," Rachel said with a smile. "I love Millville."

Jay stared at her for a long moment. His eyes

were so blue she could feel herself being pulled into their liquid depths. She forced her gaze from his, her heart fluttering in her chest.

"You really like it here?"

His tone was so incredulous that Rachel laughed out loud. The sound eased the strange tension gripping her.

"I do," she said. "Of course that doesn't mean I appreciate Mrs. Kellogg peering through her curtains to see what time Tom brings me home and how long he stays. Or Jeanie at the post office always asking me what's in a letter or who sent the priority package."

Jay grinned and shook his head. "I can't believe Jeanie Carmichael is still behind the counter. I swear the old hag was a hundred years old when I was a kid."

Rachel plopped down in the chair opposite him. "Face it, Jay—nothing really changes in Millville."

"You've changed," he said suddenly, unexpectedly, staring at her with an intensity that took her breath away. "You're all grown up and beautiful."

Rachel cursed the warmth stealing its way up her neck. It was a line Jay had probably used on a thousand girls since he'd left Millville. Most of them probably fell for it, too, but Rachel knew better. Her sister Mary had the market cornered on beautiful in her family.

"You must be running a fever." Rachel rose to her feet. "Because the last thing in the world I am is beautiful."

The last thing in the world I am is beautiful.

The words hung in the air and Jay wondered if Rachel was serious or just fishing for another compliment.

"I beg to differ," Jay said finally. "I told my mom to find me the best-looking woman in town and you were the one she chose."

Rachel laughed. "Mrs. Gibbons was the only other applicant. Need I say more?"

Jay's eyes widened. "Mrs. Gibbons who works at the nursing home?"

"Mrs. Gibbons, who *used* to work at the nursing home," Rachel clarified. "Now she *lives* there."

A skeptical look crossed Jay's face. "I can't believe my mother seriously considered her."

Rachel smiled. "She was actually the frontrunner until your mother realized she'd graduated with your aunt Lena and would need more care than you would. That's when I surged into the lead."

Jay had been prepared to tolerate Rachel. He

didn't remember much about her from school, other than she'd been standoffish with a superior air. He hadn't known she had a quirky sense of humor or such pretty blue eyes.

He let his gaze linger, glad that for whatever reason his mother had chosen her. If he had to be stuck on a farm in the middle of nowhere he might as well be stuck here with a beautiful woman.

Rachel's facial bones were delicately carved, her mouth full and he'd seen enough bleached California blondes to know that her silvery blond hair was the real deal. While her lithe figure might not be like the surgically enhanced women he'd dated in L.A., he found the natural curves oddly appealing.

Her khaki shorts and tank top flattered her figure and just looking at the creamy expanse of skin sent his pulse rate soaring. Jay grinned. For the first time since the accident he felt like himself again.

"It's good to see you smile," she said approvingly. "You must be feeling better."

"I am," he said. "And it's all because of you."

Chapter Two

Rachel's heart skipped a beat and heat rose up her neck. She'd taken this job because she needed the money. All she had to do was some light housekeeping, shuttle Jay to and from his doctor appointments and keep an eye on Aunt Lena. In return, she'd earn enough money to replace her old furnace before winter hit.

When her friends had teased her about spending so much time with "Mr. *GQ*," Rachel had only laughed. She had a steady boyfriend and even if she didn't, she was hardly the guy's type. Never in her wildest dreams had she envisioned Jay being a problem.

"If you're hungry," Rachel said pleasantly, determined not to overreact, "I could make you a fruit smoothie. The Vitamin C in the orange juice would probably be good for—"

"Rachel." His deep voice sent a shiver up her spine. "I don't want a smoothie."

She sighed. "Then what is it you *do* want, Jay?"

He stared for a long moment before his lips lifted in an easy smile.

"Fresh air," Jay said.

The twinkle in his eye said he found her discomfort amusing. Her fingers itched to pick up one of his mother's crocheted sofa pillows and throw it at his smiling face, but when he met her gaze, the look in his eye kicked her heart into overdrive and everything else was forgotten.

"When I see something I want, I go for it," Jay said. "How 'bout you?"

"I think acting in haste is never wise," Rachel said, surprised that one little look could have had such an effect on her. "Fast isn't always better. But I'm sure you already know that. After all, wasn't it speed that put you in your current predicament?"

Jay's smile vanished. "What did my mother tell you?"

Rachel shifted uncomfortably from one foot to the other, regretting the impulsive dig. Twyla Nordstrom loved to talk, and sometimes she told more than she should. But she was a lovely woman, and Rachel certainly didn't want to cause any trouble between her and her son. "Just something about you liking to drive fast."

Actually, she'd said that Jay's "heavy foot" had been the reason for the accident, but Rachel saw no need to elaborate.

"The roads were wet." Jay shrugged. "I miscalculated a hairpin turn. The tree came up out of nowhere."

Rachel shuddered at the image. "You could easily have been killed."

"When I woke up and saw myself in a mirror," Jay said, "I wished I had been."

Rachel stared in disbelief. The clearness of his gaze said he was serious.

"There's more to a person than physical beauty," she said, hastening to add, "not that you're ugly or anything now."

His lips quirked up in a humorless smile. "In my line of work, how you look can be just as important as how well you deliver the news."

"But you'll be able to go back to your old life, won't you?" Even though it had only been a few weeks, the scar's redness had already started to fade and it was easy to believe that with a little makeup, it wouldn't be visible at all. The fracture of his cheekbone would take a bit longer, but Twyla had said that Jay's plastic surgeon anticipated a complete recovery.

"I hope so," he said, "but in my business people have short memories. By the time I'm ready to go back, they might decide they like my replacement better and I'll be out."

"There are no guarantees," Rachel reluctantly agreed. She wished she could be more reassuring but his concerns were valid. "But change isn't all bad. When I was in Chicago I worked for a large firm doing training. After only eight months I was downsized. At the time I was devastated, but I realize now it was the best thing that could have happened."

"Really?" Jay leaned back in his chair, his casted arm resting on a pillow. "You liked being unemployed?"

"Of course not," Rachel said, "but the experience forced me to reevaluate my life. Only then did I realize what was really important."

"You had an epiphany."

"Exactly." Rachel nodded. "I'd gone to Chicago for all the wrong reasons. And, if I hadn't been downsized I would have stayed for all the wrong reasons."

"I'm surprised you moved there in the first

place," Jay said. "You don't seem like a big-city kind of girl to me."

Once Rachel would have been offended by the comment, but she'd learned a lot about herself during that brief stint in the Windy City. "I went to Chicago to prove to myself that I could be successful in the eyes of the world."

"Then…" he prompted when she didn't continue.

"Then it hit me that my life shouldn't be about what others thought—it should be about what *I* thought." Rachel slipped into the chair opposite Jay and the words tumbled past her lips. "I realized that while training adults to be better managers is a good thing, it isn't nearly as important as making a difference in the life of a child. As a first-grade teacher, I plant seeds that will bloom for years to come. I set the stage for the rest of their education. I—"

Rachel stopped after seeing the smile forming on his lips. An uncomfortable warmth made its way up her neck. She'd returned to Millville two years ago with her passion for teaching restored. Now she didn't just teach, she advocated for her pupils, she championed educational causes and she gave 110 percent every day. But sometimes, her renewed enthusiasm caused her to go a bit overboard. "All I'm saying is losing that job was the best thing that could have ever happened to me."

"I'm happy it worked out for you," Jay said mildly, "but I like my job and I hope it's still there when I'm ready to return."

"God willing, it will be," Rachel said.

"General manager willing is more like it," Jay said with a wry smile. "This is one decision God won't have much say in."

Rachel just shook her head. It was amazing that despite going to church all those years, Jay could be so blind regarding God's role in his life. Even she could see that Jay's accident and his return to Millville was part of some bigger plan. What that plan was, she couldn't say, but she was sure that in time all would be revealed.

Jay took a bite of the ham sandwich Rachel had packed and decided that communing with nature definitely had some benefits.

The fresh air stimulated his appetite, which had been depressed since the accident, and just getting out of that dreary old farmhouse had improved his mood. Best of all, the pond on his family's property was secluded, which meant he didn't have to worry about unexpected visitors.

Come to think of it, he'd always been able to count on the pond when he'd wanted privacy.

"What are you smiling about?" Rachel took a sip of her soda and leaned back against the trunk of a large cottonwood.

"I was remembering how I used to bring my dates here," Jay said. "It was usually so dark all you could see were stars."

"I imagine it *was* pretty—" Rachel's brows pulled together "—but why did you come all the way down here? You can see the same stars from the farmyard or from the road."

"Think about it. If I parked the car in the farm-yard, my mom would have been out of the house in a shot, and if it was parked on the side of the road, it's a given one of the sheriff's deputies would make an appearance." Jay chuckled. "I didn't want to be interrupted."

"Definitely not," Rachel said quickly.

Jay repositioned his leg on the blanket they'd spread on the ground and tried to get comfortable. The leg itself didn't hurt but his ribs had taken a beating in the accident and were still sore.

"Are you okay?" Rachel placed her can of soda on the dusty ground and concern filled her gaze.

"Couldn't be better." Jay smiled, ignoring the stabbing pain across his midsection.

But the smile must not have been very convincing because Rachel's brows drew together. She chewed on her lower lip, suddenly pensive. "Maybe bringing you out here wasn't such a good idea."

"I'm glad we did," he said emphatically. He leaned forward and impulsively took her hands in his. "I was going stir-crazy in that house."

Her skin was soft and smooth and though he'd never thought of his hands as being particularly large, hers felt positively tiny in comparison.

Rachel lowered her gaze and stared at the intertwined hands. "Jay—" She started to speak, then stopped, cleared her throat and tried again.

"What?" he said with as innocent a look as he could muster.

She stared into his eyes and for a moment he was reminded of Mrs. Ziemer, his kindergarten teacher, and the way she used to look at him when he'd insist he hadn't been the one talking in the back of the room.

Sensing defeat, he gave in to the inevitable, released his grip, and lifted his hands in a gesture of surrender. "Hands are off."

"And hands need to stay off," she said in a tone that

brooked no argument. "Remember, I have a boy-friend."

He searched her face and his admiration for her inched up a notch when he realized she was serious. Her loyalty was refreshing. And rare. Jay could count on one hand the number of women he'd met in the past five years who knew the meaning of the word fidelity.

Take Lindsay, for example. Even though they'd been dating regularly for the past six months, she hadn't called once since he left the hospital and he had the feeling she'd already moved on to greener pastures.

Still, he could be giving Rachel too much credit. It might not be loyalty at all. It could be that she didn't find him attractive and was using Tom as an excuse. The thought was too depressing to consider. Better to give her the benefit of the doubt and believe she really was committed to Tom.

Even though he and Tom had once been best friends, Jay hadn't thought of the guy in years. He wondered if Tom still went overboard when he was in love. As a teen, Tom's single-minded devotion had made him popular with the ladies.

He'd been a generous guy with a quirky sense of humor whose only weakness had been a temper that would flare without warning. Jay still remembered the time Tom had gone ballistic over nothing and slammed Karen against the wall. Karen had been shaken by the experience and had told him she never wanted to see him again.

But it wasn't long until Tom had wheedled his way back in her good graces and they'd eventually married.

"Your devotion to Tom is refreshing," Jay said.

"Tom is very good to me." Rachel lifted her chin in a gesture that seemed to dare him to say otherwise. "We have a great relationship."

"I would hope so," Jay said, wondering about the slight hitch in her voice. "Otherwise what's the point?"

Chapter Three

Rachel returned home that night to find a big bouquet of flowers waiting. Unfortunately the attached love note from Tom only served to remind her of something she'd been doing her best to forget.

Three months ago when Tom had first asked her out, Rachel had been over the moon with happiness. After that first date she'd seen him every day. Up until a couple of weeks ago Rachel had felt she'd known him better than most of her friends.

He was such a romantic, always sending her flowers and love poems, and giving her little gifts. And unlike many men who seemed happier spending time with the guys, Tom wanted to be with *her*.

When her friend Jocelyn had said it would drive her absolutely crazy if Adam, her husband, wanted to spend so much time with her, Rachel had only smiled. She liked running errands with Tom, fixing dinner for him in the evening and attending church together on Sunday. Though her friends complained they never saw her anymore, Rachel had loved her life as Tom's girlfriend.

Her gaze shifted to the flowers. She'd never seen such huge spider mums. The colorful flowers were her favorite and it was so like Tom to make sure the florist sent the very best. She inhaled their fragrant scent.

I'm making too much out of nothing, she told herself. Tom is a great guy and I'm a lucky woman. Besides, he's said over and over he's sorry and he's promised it will never happen again.

But he said that before, a little voice whispered, and it *did* happen again.

A tear slipped down Rachel's cheek. A second one followed. Maybe what her father had said way back in high school was true, maybe she did bring out the worst in a man. After all, Tom insisted that nothing like this had ever happened before.

Rachel knew she could be opinionated and headstrong, but she'd always thought of herself as a good listener and someone willing to compromise. But after the second incident she'd given Tom an ultimatum: get counseling or it was over.

Tom had tried to convince her that seeing a psychologist would just be a waste of time. He didn't need to pay someone to tell him what he'd already figured out: when they were arguing he just needed to keep his hands off her. Problem solved.

The first time Rachel had backed down, but this time she'd insisted. Tom hadn't been happy, but he'd finally agreed when he'd realized she was serious. Rachel glanced at the clock. Tom's first counseling session should be over by now.

As if on cue, the phone rang.

Rachel wiped the tears from her cheeks with the back of her hand and hurried into the living room. She grabbed the cordless phone and plopped into an overstuffed chair. "Hello."

"I'm glad you're home," Tom said. "Did you get my flowers?"

"They're beautiful." Rachel tried to put some enthusiasm into her voice. "And the note was very sweet."

"I meant what I said," Tom said. "I'm so sorry I hurt you and I'll spend the rest of my life making it up to you."

Actions speak louder than words.

Rachel could almost hear mother admonishing her, but Rachel reminded herself that Tom *was* doing something.

"How did the counseling session go?" she asked, eager for news about the session. "Did you like Dr. Peters? Do you think the two of you will work well together?"

Tom didn't answer immediately and as a long moment of silence filled the other end of the phone line, dread coursed through Rachel. Her fingers tightened around the receiver.

"I didn't go," he said finally. "We had some problems at the bank and I couldn't get away."

Rachel's chest constricted. She took a deep breath and forced herself to remain calm. *Problems.* She clung to the word. Maybe the bank had been robbed. Maybe an employee had gotten locked in a vault. Maybe he *did* have a good excuse. She wasn't going to jump to conclusions. "What kind of problems?"

"Lots of things," he hedged. "They'll probably sound like nothing to you."

She switched the phone to her other hand and wiped her sweaty right palm against her shorts. "Try me."

"C'mon, Rach." Tom's tone turned persuasive. "We've got a good thing going. I don't need some two-bit shrink telling me how to behave. I promise, I'll treat you like the princess you are for the rest of my life. You just wait and see."

Empty promises, her mother's voice whispered. Every time her mother had threatened to leave, her father had promised to change. He never had.

"You said you'd see a counselor." Rachel didn't even try to keep the disappointment from her voice.

"Well, you've promised me a lot of things you haven't followed through on, either," he said.

"Like what?"

"Like when you said you'd go to a baseball game in Chicago with me," he said. "We've never done that."

"We never found a time that worked for both of us," Rachel said, her irritation surging at this blatant attempt to change the subject. "It's hardly the same thing."

"Maybe not to you," he said.

Was it possible for a heart to break in two? At the moment it seemed highly likely.

Rachel drew a ragged breath and straightened her shoulders. "I can't do this anymore, Tom. It's no good."

"Rach, don't do this. I love you. I—"

Rachel could hear the panic in his tone and knew

the promises were ready to start. But this time she wasn't interested in promises.

His actions had already said it all.

The next morning Rachel woke to the sound of rain beating against her window. When she opened her blinds and saw only grey dreariness, it somehow seemed fitting. Despite knowing she'd had no choice but to break off her relationship with Tom, the thought of being without him made her heart ache.

Somehow Rachel found a way to make it through that day and the ones that followed. Instead of leaving right when Jay's father, Henry, came in from the fields, Rachel waited until supper was finished and the dishes done before heading home.

Every day she put on a happy face and did her best to hide her heartache. By Friday she felt confident she'd been successful.

But though Jay wasn't always the most observant guy, he'd noticed the change in Rachel's mood. And by the end of the week he realized that not only hadn't she spoken of her boyfriend all week, she'd changed the subject whenever Jay brought Tom up.

While his father and Lena retired to the living room to read the paper, Jay stayed in the kitchen with Rachel. He watched her wipe down the kitchen countertops and decided the time had come to find out what was going on. "You and Tom have big plans for the weekend?"

Though her back was to him, Jay could see her shoulders tense. "I don't really have any plans except coming here on Saturday and going to church on Sunday."

Since his father didn't believe in working on the Sabbath, Sunday had been designated as Rachel's day off. When his mother had come up with the arrangement before she'd left for Texas, Jay had wondered how he was going to stand having some stranger around six out of seven days. Now, he wondered how he was going to stand not seeing Rachel on Sunday.

"Do you and Tom attend church together?" Jay asked, keeping his tone conversational.

"We both go to First Christian," she said.

"That's not what I asked." Jay forced a teasing note into the words.

Rachel turned and met his gaze. "Are you on a fishing expedition?"

Jay thought about playing dumb, but he'd never particularly liked beating around the bush or been particularly good at it. "Are you and Tom having problems?"

She rested her back against the counter, her expression inscrutable. "Why do you ask?"

Jay shrugged. "When you came back on Tuesday, you seemed down. I guessed you and Tom had probably just had a fight. But it's Friday and you don't seem any happier."

"I'm perfectly hap-py." Her voice broke on the last word and tears welled up in her big blue eyes, slipping silently down her cheek.

Jay shifted in the kitchen chair and cursed his curiosity. He'd never meant to make her cry.

Rachel hurriedly reached into her pocket and pulled out a tissue, her cheeks bright pink. "I'm sorry."

"You don't have to explain," Jay reassured her, hoping to forestall any further tears. "What goes on between you and Tom is your business, not mine."

"We broke up." Rachel sniffed and dabbed at her eyes with the tissue.

Jay pulled his brows together. "I'm sure you'll make up."

"Not this time." Heavy resignation hung in her voice and her lips drooped down like a sad clown.

Jay wanted nothing more than to pull her into his arms and soothe her hurt, but he settled for a sympathetic expression. "What happened?"

She shifted her gaze to the window behind him. "Some old problems resurfaced. I told him it was over."

"*You* broke up with *him*?" Jay couldn't hide his surprise. As sad as Rachel looked, he'd assumed Tom had dumped her.

Rachel nodded.

"I'm sure he'll make amends," Jay said. "The Tom Tidball I remember isn't the type of guy to just walk away and give up."

Rachel sighed. "Oh, he's not giving up. My house has so many flowers, it looks like a funeral parlor and since I won't answer his calls on my cell, he fills up my recorder at home."

Jay met her gaze. "Sounds like the guy is in love and doesn't want to lose you."

"I don't know about the love part—" Rachel glanced away "—but he's already lost me."

Despite not knowing the circumstances, Jay couldn't help but feel sorry for Tom. "Can't you give him another chance?"

She lifted her chin. "He's had his chance."

Jay stared at Rachel for a long moment. Though she seemed firm in her resolve, the pain in her eyes told him this hadn't been an easy decision. "Is there anything I can do?"

"There's nothing anyone can do," Rachel said.

It was going to be awkward for her, Jay realized. Breakups in a small town were never easy. When he and Kim had broken up at the end of his senior year, it had been mutual. But seeing her had still been hard.

"It's too bad you don't live in a big city," Jay said, only half-joking. "You'd never have to see him again."

"That *would* be a blessing." A smile lifted her lips before vanishing as quickly as it had appeared. "I dread church on Sunday. I know he'll be there, wanting to sit with me, begging me to reconsider."

"Don't go." Jay thought the suggestion made good sense, but the look on her face told him she didn't agree.

"Tom can be so charming, so persuasive," Rachel said, almost to herself. "And he has so many wonderful qualities."

"Have you talked to the minister about the situation?"

From what she'd told him, Rachel was very involved at First Christian and really liked the pastor.

"Why would I do that?" She met his gaze head on. "I'm not changing my mind."

"I'm not saying you should," Jay hastened to

clarify. "I just thought it might make you feel better about your decision if you talked about it with someone you trusted."

"I'm not sure anything will make me feel better," Rachel said, "but I'll consider your suggestion."

"Is the word out?"

"Out?"

"Do people in town know you two broke up?"

"I told my friends on Tuesday," Rachel said. "I'm sure the news has gotten around."

"You told them on Tuesday but you didn't mention it to me until today." Jay paused. "Why?"

Rachel shrugged. "Just don't feel like talking about it."

He didn't believe it for a minute, but he let the remark go unchallenged. "So, what's next?"

Rachel sighed. "My next hurdle is Sunday."

"Go to church with your mom," he suggested. The last he knew her mother still lived in Millville. Jay remembered her father as a stern man who'd once banned him from the town's only grocery store. He'd died in a car accident during Rachel's senior year in high school. Her mother had been a quiet woman who seemed friendly enough, but never said much. "I assume she still lives in town?"

"My mother is spending the month in Kansas

City helping my sister with her second baby,"
Rachel said.

"Maybe one of your friends—"

"I'll be fine, really," she said, then paused. "Un-less…"

Jay raised a brow. "Unless?"

"Unless you'd consider going with me?"

Chapter Four

Jay started to laugh. He knew it was bad form, but he couldn't stop himself. The only reason he was in Millville was because the farm was so isolated he didn't need to see anyone. Showing up at church would be the equivalent of signing on to be a sideshow attraction at the county fair. "No way."

Her face reddened as if she'd been slapped and she spun on her heel, turning her attention to the already clean counter. "Forget I asked. I just thought if you wanted to get out of the hou—" She stopped. "It was a stupid idea."

Her shoulders were stiff and Jay realized with a start that he'd offended her.

Using the table as leverage, Jay pushed himself up to a standing position and hobbled across the room to where Rachel stood scrubbing a nonexistent spot from the Formica. He rested his good hand on her shoulder and felt her muscles tense beneath his touch.

"It wasn't a stupid idea," he said, his fingers massaging her shoulder, "but church is the last place I want to be right now."

"I shouldn't have asked." She turned and met his gaze, her eyes hooded. "Tom isn't your concern—he's mine."

Something in the way she spoke sent red flags popping up in his head. "If he hassles you at all, I want to know."

This time it was Rachel's turn to laugh. "What are you going to do? Hit him with your cast?"

Irritation surged through Jay.

"I mean it, Rachel." Jay could still see the look of fear in Karen's eyes when he'd pulled Tom off of her. "You let me know."

"I will," Rachel promised. Before he knew what was happening, she leaned forward and planted a kiss on his cheek. "Thanks."

The light, flowery scent of her perfume filled his nostrils and stirred his senses. Jay reacted instinctively, pulling her close.

But before his lips could cover hers, she turned her head and his kiss brushed her jaw.

"This isn't right," she whispered against his chest.

"You're not with Tom anymore," Jay reminded her.

"I'm not ready for another relationship." She pulled away and lifted her large blue eyes to his. "I'm sorry."

Relationship? Jay barely hid his surprise. Since when did a kiss mean anything more than, well, you were attracted to a person and wanted to show it?

"I understand," he said finally, a knot forming in his stomach as the realization hit.

Though doubt flickered in her eyes, Jay wished there was some way he could assure her that he really did understand. Lindsay had made it perfectly clear that he no longer held any appeal when she'd hightailed it out of his hospital room. The only thing that surprised him was that he'd considered for even a moment that Rachel might be different.

Monday morning Rachel had barely made it into the foyer of the Nordstrom's two-story farmhouse when Jay hobbled into view.

"How was yesterday?" His gaze searched hers. "Did Tom cause any problems?"

His obvious concern warmed her heart. When she'd left on Saturday she'd been certain he wouldn't give her or her problems a second thought. But she didn't want to even think about yesterday until she'd had some caffeine.

"Why don't we go into the kitchen and talk? I'll make us some coffee." She tilted her head and sniffed the air. Something smelled awfully good. "Unless you already have some brewing?"

"There's just some leftover stuff Dad made at five-thirty," Jay said. "It's black as mud."

Rachel smiled at the disgust in his voice and slipped past him on her way to the kitchen. As she brushed against him she realized that the delicious scent she'd smelled a few moments ago hadn't been flavored coffee, but was Jay's cologne.

The spicy fragrance stirred her senses and her heart picked up speed. Not only did Jay smell good, he looked good.

The blue chambray shirt he wore accentuated his eyes and his blond hair was tousled as if he'd just got out of bed.

But as appealing as she found him, Rachel had decided last night that her best course of action would be to keep Jay at arm's length. So she drew a steadying breath, ordered her heart to return to a normal rhythm and forced her attention to the matter at hand. "I'll take that comment to mean you'd like me to make some fresh?"

"You bet." He flashed a boyish smile. "Especially if I could get some bacon and eggs to go with it."

Rachel laughed. "Bacon and eggs it is."

Thirty minutes later, Lena was on the porch sipping her tea while Rachel sat at the table watching Jay finish off the last of the bacon.

"That omelet was fabulous," Jay said. "And the bacon was perfect."

A flush of pleasure traveled through Rachel and she couldn't help but smile. "I'm glad you liked it."

Jay wiped the corners of his mouth with the napkin and leaned back in his chair. "Now, tell me how Sunday went."

They'd talked about everything but her and Tom while she'd prepared breakfast. And, even after the food was ready, Jay had kept the conversation light. Only now, after they'd both finished, did he bring up the subject again.

She supposed she should be flattered that he was interested in her life, but the truth was, discussing personal issues with Jay made her a bit uneasy.

"You're Tom's friend," Rachel said, trying to be

diplomatic. "I'm not sure I should be talking about him to you."

"I *was* his friend, but that was a long time ago." Jay reached across the table and took her hand. "Now I'm *your* friend."

The touch of his hand sent a shock of electricity up her arm. She pulled her hand away and reined in her emotions. Arm's length, she reminded herself, taking a quick sip of coffee.

"Tom showed up at the church," she said in a remarkably calm tone. "I was already seated when suddenly there he was, next to me in the pew."

"Sounds like a soap opera," Jay said lightly, but she could see the concern in his eyes. "Did you cause a scene?"

Rachel shot him a reproachful glance. "Do I look like the type of person who'd cause a disturbance in God's house?"

Jay appeared to ponder the question for a minute, then grinned. "Yep."

Rachel couldn't help but laugh. "Well, I didn't. I kept my gaze focused on Pastor Karelli and my thoughts on the sermon."

"Somehow," Jay said, "I don't believe it was as easy as all that."

"Why do you say that?"

She'd expected him to toss off some one-liner about knowing her so well even though it had only been a week, but instead his gaze turned serious.

"Because I've been there before."

"You have?" She couldn't keep the surprise from her voice.

"One of my first jobs in California was in this small station just outside of San Francisco," he said with a faint smile. "Christy was a meteorologist. I used to call her my weather girl."

Rachel couldn't remember his mother ever mentioning a Christy, so either the romance was short-lived or he'd never told his mom about the woman.

"What happened?"

"Our relationship was like fireworks, hot while it lasted but burning out quickly," he said. "Though we parted amicably, being together in the same studio became extremely awkward. Our co-workers knew we'd been involved and they were always watching us to see if there was any spark left."

"That's exactly what happened yesterday." The church service had been the longest of Rachel's life. "But it was worse because, although I don't want to be with Tom anymore, I still like him."

The smell of Tom's cologne, the feel of his strong

arm pressed next to hers, the endearing way he sang off-key had all tugged at her heart.

"Did you two talk?"

Rachel shook her head. "Not really. After the service he asked if I'd go out to lunch with him so we could discuss what happened, but I said no."

"How did he take your refusal?"

"He told me he was sure we could work things out, but for that to happen we needed to communicate." She sighed and shook her head. "He just doesn't get it. There's no point in talking. It's over."

"Tom always was doggedly persistent," Jay said. "You're probably going to have to be involved with someone else before he'll back off."

"Well, that's not going to happen," Rachel said with a wry smile. "I'm steering clear of men for a while. I'm not ready for another relationship."

"I'm not talking about a relationship," Jay said. "I'm talking dating someone just so Tom will back off."

"I could never use anyone like that."

"It wouldn't be using if they knew and agreed to the charade."

"Well, it's a moot point anyway, because you know as well as I do that everyone in this town is already hooked up."

"Not everyone," Jay said.

"You show me one eligible guy under Medicare age," Rachel said and then added, "who'd be crazy enough to go along with such a scheme and I'll consider it."

"I can name one guy off the top of my head."

Rachel decided to call Jay's bluff. "Okay, name him."

Jay smiled. "Me."

"You?" Rachel burst out laughing. "Nobody would ever believe that you and I were dating, least of all Tom."

Her laughter surprised him. Though Jay knew he looked awful, no one else in town had seen him. "Because of the way I look?"

"No," she said, her smile dimming. "Because of the way *I* look."

"What's wrong with the way you look?" From where he sat, she looked absolutely lovely. Oh, her simple cotton blouse and jean shorts weren't going to win any fashion awards, but she'd done something different with her hair—pulling it back in a couple of clips—and her blue eyes were the same shade as the June sky. Her lips were rosy and full and he decided kissing her would be the perfect dessert to a bacon and eggs breakfast.

"—not like my sister Mary."

Jay realized with a start that while he'd been day-dreaming, words had been flowing from those delectable lips. "What about your sister?"

Rachel heaved an exasperated sigh. "Weren't you listening to a word I said?"

He thought about telling her he'd been too busy sizing her up to listen, but decided to play it safe. "Are we talking about the Mary Tanner who gradu-ated a year before me?"

The one he was visualizing had large breasts, mousy brown hair and an irritating laugh.

"That's my sister," Rachel said. "Mary is the pretty one in the family."

Although it had to be the same person, average rather than pretty was a word he'd use to describe the girl. But Rachel was speaking in the present tense, so perhaps her sister had been a late bloomer.

"From what I can remember," Jay said honestly, "you're a lot prettier."

"That's sweet of you to say," Rachel said, "but it's not necessary."

Now she'd lost him completely. He wasn't being

sweet, he was being honest. And he still didn't understand why she wasn't jumping all over his offer.

"I'd be a good pretend boyfriend," he said. The fact was he'd probably be a better pretend boyfriend than a real one.

She studied him for a moment, then pushed back her chair and stood. "I'm sure you would. But if I ever have another boyfriend, I want him to be someone who really cares for me, not someone who pretends."

Jay digested her words. It appeared she might have inadvertently shared what had gone wrong between her and Tom. Obviously Tom had just been stringing her along and then when she found out what he was doing, she'd broken it off.

Still, it didn't explain why Tom was trying so hard to get her back. Unless he'd turned into a guy who only wanted what he couldn't have. If that was the case, Rachel had been wise to move slowly.

"So you don't need anything from me?" Jay asked.

"I need you to be my friend," Rachel said.

"I can do that." Though he'd never played that role, Jay knew he could pull it off.

Although he couldn't recall a single girl who'd been just a friend, growing up he'd had plenty of guy friends and he was a quick study. He could learn to be a good friend because he had the feeling that if he did, this summer might not be nearly as boring as he'd anticipated. Especially if he could convince Rachel that "friendly" kissing was just what the doctor ordered.

Chapter Five

Jay's father returned to the living room and held out a cigar. "Want one?"

Rachel had already headed home for the evening and Lena had retired to her room, leaving the two men alone. In the short time Jay had been back, he and his father had settled into an evening routine. Jay would read or watch television while his father smoked a cigar and glanced through the newspaper.

They rarely talked. Henry Nordstrom was a man of few words. Besides, he and Jay had little in common.

"Do you want one or not?" His father's brusque tone brought Jay back to the present.

"No, thanks." Jay looked up from his book and wondered idly why his father continued to ask. In all the weeks since he'd come home, he hadn't once said yes.

"Suit yourself." Henry shrugged and flicked a match, lighting the thick stogie. He puffed contentedly for several minutes in silence. "Did I mention some of my old army buddies are getting together in Des Moines this weekend?"

"That should be a good time," Jay said without any real enthusiasm. He'd never understood the need to mingle with those from the past. Once a part of your life was over, he believed it was best to move on and not look back.

His dad shifted his gaze from the newspaper and his eyes took on a distant, faraway look. "Mossy is coming all the way from Wisconsin."

Jay wasn't sure who Mossy was but obviously he was a friend. He'd never really thought of his father having friends. It was an interesting concept. Henry had always seemed like such a loner.

His father brought the cigar to his lips then exhaled a large cloud of smoke. "I need to call and let them know I won't be there."

"You're not going?" Jay couldn't keep the surprise from his voice.

"Crops to get in." His father flicked a smattering of ashes into a sauce dish he'd confiscated from the china hutch. "They're talking rain all next week."

It was all Jay could do not to groan. When he was growing up, family activities had been scheduled around the weather. A decade later and it sounded as if that hadn't changed.

"Rain isn't in the forecast until Wednesday," Jay reminded him. "You'll be back before then."

"I'd be home on Sunday," Henry said. "If I go, that is."

"Just hit it extra hard when you get back," Jay said.

His father never took a vacation and rarely even took a day off. The man was due some R and R.

"I might be able to make it work with the planting," his father grudgingly admitted, "but what about you? And your aunt Lena? I can't leave you alone with her."

Jay's heart warmed under his father's concern. When his mother had called, insisting he come home to recuperate, Jay had hesitated. Easter had been painful. His father had treated him as a guest he didn't know what to do with and Jay had ended up counting the hours until he could return to L.A.

"I can take care of myself," Jay said. "And Lena, too. Don't worry about me."

"It's not you I'm worried about." Henry placed

his cigar in the sauce dish. "It's your mother. She'd skin me alive if something happened and she found out I'd left you and Lena alone."

A twinge of disappointment tugged at Jay, before he reminded himself he'd been crazy to think his father would worry about *him*.

"Go," Jay said with a wave. "I can take care of myself."

"You *are* getting around better—" a thoughtful look crossed his father's face before he shook his head "—but if you fall, Lena won't be of much help."

"I won't fall," Jay said with more confidence than he felt.

"I don't know…." His father rubbed his chin with his hand.

"What if Rachel stayed?" Jay asked, wondering why the solution hadn't occurred to him before. "Would that make you feel better?"

His father straightened in his chair. "Would she do that?"

"She'd do anything I asked." Even to Jay's own ears the words sounded cocky and arrogant, but they were said, and he couldn't take them back.

Henry's gaze narrowed. "What do you mean by that crack?"

The censure in his father's tone quashed any desire Jay might have had about backing off from the statement.

"Rachel likes me." Jay met his father's gaze, not a hint of apology in his tone.

"You best remember Rachel Tanner is a God-fearing woman, a teacher, a respected member of our community." Henry pointed a finger at Jay. "She's not one of your Los Angeles floozies."

Jay stared silently at his father and a sadness he couldn't control washed over him. His father had never approved of his career choice or his lifestyle. And though he'd been pleasant to Lindsay when they'd met, obviously he hadn't approved of her, either.

"I'm not going to take advantage of Rachel, if that's what you're worried about," Jay said. "Though I don't see where it's any of your concern."

Henry leaned forward, steel in his gaze. "This is my home. And while Rachel is a guest in my home, you'll treat her with the respect she deserves. Is that understood?"

Though Jay resented his father's lecturing tone, he couldn't help but respect him for standing up for Rachel. Most people Jay knew only cared about themselves.

"I promise," Jay said, adopting a conciliatory tone. "You don't have anything to worry about."

Henry's gaze lingered on his son for a long moment, before he leaned back, seemingly satisfied. "That girl had a hard life, growing up with a father like Frank Tanner. I don't want to see it made even harder."

Jay took a sip of his cola. "Didn't Frank die in a car accident?"

Henry nodded and took another leisurely puff on his cigar, blowing little smoke rings in the air. It was as if he were determined to enjoy the experience to the fullest knowing the cigars would be relegated to special occasions once his wife returned. "Darned fool rolled his car on gravel. Always did drive too fast."

Something stirred in the back of Jay's memory. "You two were in school together, weren't you?"

Henry nodded. "We were friends through high school, but not so much after."

"How come?"

"Frank went off to college," Henry said. "I stayed here and farmed, but even when he moved back and started the grocery, it wasn't the same between us. He'd changed. Or maybe I had."

"Sort of like Wayne and I," Jay said, thinking of how close he and his brother had been as children and how little in common they had now.

"That's different," Henry said. "You and Wayne are family. There will always be that bond between you."

Jay stared into the unlit fireplace. "I don't fit in here."

"Stop with that kind of talk," Henry said in a gruff tone, and only then did Jay realize he'd spoken aloud.

"What about your get-together?" Jay asked, quickly changing the subject. "Are you going to go or not?"

"Are you sure Rachel won't mind staying?"

"She won't mind at all."

"And I can trust the two of you to keep out of trouble. Right?"

Jay smiled. "Absolutely."

Rachel slid into the chair, relieved when the young minister took the chair adjacent to hers rather than sitting behind the desk. "Thanks for seeing me, Pastor."

If Tony Karelli found it odd that Rachel didn't call him by his first name, he didn't mention it. "Anytime. That's what I'm here for."

His smile was friendly and Rachel couldn't help but remember the first time she'd seen him. At the time she'd just moved back to Millville and Tony had been in town less than a month. When she'd run into the handsome stranger on one of the outdoor running trails and he'd gone out of his way to put her at ease, Rachel had wondered if this could be the man of her dreams. Unfortunately, her hopes had been quickly dashed when she'd discovered he was engaged.

"How is Claire? And the baby?" she asked, realizing she hadn't yet made it over to the house to see their new family member.

"Jacob is four weeks old today," Tony said proudly of his first child. "And Claire is absolutely gaga over him. Of course, she always did have a thing for guys."

Rachel laughed and the tension that had gripped her when she'd thought of this meeting eased. "I bet she's a wonderful mother."

"We're both learning." Tony smiled ruefully. "And Mrs. Sandy is a gem. She's already helped us through some rough spots."

Mrs. Sandy ran a bed-and-breakfast in Millville and had been Tony's landlady when he'd first moved to town. She'd quickly become Tony and Claire's surrogate mother.

"We all need a little help now and then," Rachel murmured.

"You're exactly right." Tony reached over and covered her hand with his. "I know you were apprehensive about coming and talking to me but I want you to remember what you just said, because it's true. We all need help now and then. I'm here for you. And God is here for you, too."

Rachel could feel the last of the tension leave her body and she relaxed against the back of the over-stuffed leather chair. "I don't know where to begin."

Tony's brown eyes were warm and his smile encouraging. "Start wherever you want."

Thirty minutes later she'd told the Pastor everything about her and Tom's time together, including the two incidents of physical violence that had caused her to end their relationship. "I really like Tom and given time I could have easily loved him. But I can't tolerate abuse. And Tom refuses to get help. He just keeps asking me to forgive him."

"I wish I'd known you two were having these problems." Tony's dark eyes were troubled.

"I was embarrassed," Rachel said. "And I felt guilty."

Tony raised a dark brow. "Guilty?"

"That I'd done something to cause him to behave this way," she said. "He said he's never lost control like that before."

"Rachel, this is *his* problem, not yours." Tony leaned forward in his chair, his eyes firm with conviction. "I don't care if you'd screamed obscenities in his face—there was no excuse for what he did to you."

"My father once told me I bring out the worst in a man," Rachel said.

"Your father—" Tony started, then appeared to reconsider his words. "Though I never had the pleasure of meeting him, I think your father had some issues of his own to deal with."

"So you don't think I'm wrong to not want to be with Tom anymore?" Rachel had never thought of herself as a woman who needed others to approve her actions, but this thing with Tom had shaken her confidence.

"Dating is a time to get to know each other," Tony said. "It's a time to discover if you're really meant to be together long-term."

"I could never marry someone I feared," Rachel said. "I don't want to be afraid of my own husband."

Tony opened the Bible to Ephesians and they spent the next half hour talking about what Paul had written regarding marriage and the way it should be between a man and a woman.

"So you can see," Tony finished, "that while each partner in the relationship is an individual and has an individual relationship with God, He designed each to function in perfect harmony *if* they both follow His outline. If either fails to follow His plan, the relationship is not God-centered and likely to fail."

Rachel pulled her brows together in thought, trying to process what the minister was saying. "So, you're saying that because Tom's actions weren't in accordance with God's plan, our relationship wasn't God-centered even though we both believed in God."

"That's absolutely correct. Until Tom addresses this problem he won't be a good partner for anyone." Tony closed his Bible and met her gaze. "I'd like your permission to talk to a couple of my elders about this matter and then I'd like us to approach Tom."

"I'm not going back to him," Rachel said firmly. She remembered all too well being subjected to her father's irrational tirades. There was no way she was going to live in such an abusive environment again. "It's over between us."

"I'm not advocating you two resume your relationship," Tony said, "but Tom has a problem that he has to deal with and he needs to get some help."

"I'd like to see him get help, too," Rachel said. "Talk to him. Maybe you can make a difference. For his sake, I hope so."

Chapter Six

"Turning away the ladies from the church auxiliary was downright rude." Rachel glared at Jay, her hands fisted on her hips.

"I don't like people who stop by without calling," Jay said, not seeming the least bit concerned he'd just refused to see two of the town's most respected volunteers, "but I do appreciate the cookies."

A platter of freshly baked chocolate-chip cookies sat on the table and their delicious aroma filled the large country kitchen. When Jay lifted the plastic wrap and grabbed one, Rachel was tempted to slap his hand. If he wouldn't talk to the ladies, he didn't deserve to eat their treats.

Still, it would be a shame to let such perfectly

good cookies go to waste, especially when there were starving children in Africa.

Waste not, want not had always been her mother's credo.

Rachel smiled at the thought and moved to the cupboard. She grabbed two glasses and quickly filled them with cold milk.

Returning to the table, Rachel set one glass on the table in front of Jay then took a seat opposite him. She reached for a cookie and realized while she'd been getting the milk, he'd already helped himself to two more.

Rachel felt her mood lift at the first bite.

"You're not nearly as upset as I thought you'd be," Jay mused, taking a sip of milk. "I think you don't like those two any more than I do."

After hearing her father bad-mouth other people for years, Rachel had made it a practice to keep her mouth shut unless she had something good to say. She took another bite of the cookie and evaded the question. "I could tell they realized you didn't want to see them the minute I said you were resting and couldn't be disturbed."

Jay groaned. "Tell me that's not the reason you gave."

"Hey." Rachel waved a cookie in the air. "You

were lying down and you could have been asleep. Not to mention you *didn't* want to be disturbed."

"I never cared for Mrs. Mitchell," Jay said. "Or the other one. If you ask me, neither are the charitable type."

"They put in a lot of time at the church," Rachel informed him. "That's in addition to the hours they volunteer at the schools."

"They might do some good," Jay grudgingly acknowledged, "but they were nosy busybodies back when I was a kid and I bet you ten dollars they haven't changed one bit."

Rachel wished she could refute his words, but Gladys Mitchell and Raye Cosgrove were well-known gossips. And, as much as Rachel wanted to believe their visit today was pure Christian charity, her gut told her that they'd simply come to take a gander at Jay and report back to their cohorts.

"You're probably right." Rachel took another cookie, knowing there was no "probably" about it, "but you should have let them see you. Then everyone would know that, despite his injuries, Jay Nordstrom is still an incredible hunk."

Though she'd exaggerated a bit, she was rewarded with a brief smile.

"Let me draw your attention to this." Jay touched

the red scar trailing down his cheek with the tip of one finger. "And to this hideous area around my eye, and to—"

"Okay, okay. So maybe you have a few teensy little flaws but who cares?" Rachel kept her tone deliberately light. "You're still the same arrogant guy inside."

That brought the smile back to his face and Rachel wondered if now would be the time to ask him. When he took another cookie she decided to go for it. After all, if four homemade chocolate-chip cookies weren't enough to get him in a good mood, she didn't know what would be.

Jay hadn't been off the property since he'd arrived in Millville and it was time for him to reenter society. Baby steps, she told herself. Lunch and a movie would be baby steps.

"I think you need to get out." Rachel kept her tone deliberately casual. "How about we go to Des Moines for a movie? Maybe have lunch at a nice restaurant? You've got to be sick of my cooking."

"A movie sounds good," Jay said. "I'd like to see—"

He paused before naming a movie that had been on DVD at least a year.

"I'm afraid that isn't in the theaters anymore,"

Rachel said. "The only way you're going to see that one is to rent it."

"Great idea." Jay smiled. "Pick it up when you're in town."

She narrowed her gaze. Something told her she'd played right into his hands and this was what he'd wanted all along. "No movie theater?"

He shook his head.

"No lunch at a nice restaurant?"

Jay winked. "Your cooking is every bit as good as any restaurant food."

Rachel sighed. He was incorrigible. Cute but incorrigible.

"We'll have more fun here," he said. "In fact, suddenly I can't wait for Friday night."

"You're forgetting something." Rachel softened her words with a smile. "I don't work Friday night."

"I'm glad you mentioned that," Jay said with an innocent air. "I need you to stay the weekend. Dad's old war buddies are having a reunion in Des Moines and he wasn't going until I told him you'd be happy to fill in."

Rachel started shaking her head no before he even finished. As it was now, she practically lived at the Nordstrom farm. She couldn't give up her nights and Sunday off. "Spending the night wasn't part of the deal."

"I'm sure you could use the extra cash for your furnace fund," Jay said, his tone persuasive. "Lena will be here, too, though she'll probably spend most of the time in her room. And Dad is really looking forward to the reunion."

Though his smile tugged at Rachel's resolve and the money would be nice, her laundry was piled high and her house needed a thorough cleaning. It was only the thought of Henry missing a weekend with his war buddies that stopped Rachel from saying no immediately.

"He says he won't leave Lena and me here alone," Jay added. "Even though I told him we'd make do."

Make do.

That's what most of the hardworking farmers in the area did. Henry was no exception. Ten years ago he'd been close to bankruptcy, but he'd sold off some acres and with hard work and the grace of God he'd been able to hold onto the rest of his land. It didn't take a genius to know that the event must be important for him to consider spending a weekend away from the farm, especially at this time of year.

"Okay," Rachel said, hoping she didn't regret the decision. "I'll do it."

"Great." Jay smiled broadly and, despite her resolve not to let him affect her, Rachel's heart skipped a beat. "When you get the movie, pick up something for dinner."

"Friday is meat loaf day," Rachel stammered, the look in his eyes making her blush like a schoolgirl. "It's your father's favorite."

"He won't be here and Lena isn't particular," Jay reminded her. "I'm thinking lobster or salmon would be nice for a change."

"Okay." At the moment he could have asked her to fry a squirrel and she'd have agreed. "Anything else?"

"Candles," Jay said. "If we're going to make it a special evening, we want to do it right."

"Special evening?" Now he had her thoroughly confused.

"It's our first date." Jay smiled. "I'd like it to be perfect."

"Date?" Rachel's jaw dropped. She shut it with a snap. "I just thought it'd be nice for you to get out of the house."

Jay sat back in the chair, his expression inscrutable. "You don't want to date me?"

"Absolutely not," Rachel said firmly, ignoring a niggle of doubt.

Though her tone couldn't have been more sure, a trace of a smile returned to his lips at her words. With his gaze fixed on her, Jay trailed a finger slowly along the Formica tabletop.

Rachel's gaze followed the movement and she had a sudden vivid image of those fingers traveling up her arm. Her breath quickened. He picked up another cookie and brought the sweet morsel to his mouth.

"Maybe you don't want to date me," he said, "but you sure do want to kiss me."

Her head jerked up and she discovered his gaze fixed firmly on her.

She cringed at the knowing look in his eyes. For a second she wondered if he could read her mind. She immediately dismissed the thought as ridiculous. He'd made a guess, pure and simple, and if she kept her cool and played her cards right, he'd never know he'd been right.

She attempted a look of confusion. "Where in the world did you get such a crazy idea?"

Though Rachel had never been a good actress, she might have been able to pull it off if she'd kept focused. Unfortunately, even as she denied her interest, Rachel found her gaze drawn to his lips.

"Admit it. You wonder what it would be like to kiss me."

She pulled her gaze from his mouth even as heat rose up her neck. "I do not."

His smile widened and pure masculine satisfaction filled his gaze. "Yes, you do."

Rachel heaved an exasperated sigh. Hadn't his mother taught him that a true gentleman never made a lady feel uncomfortable?

"Arrogant jerk," she muttered under her breath.

She must have spoken more loudly than she'd intended because Jay chuckled, the insult apparently only fueling his amusement. "I think you protest too much."

"You're so—" Rachel stopped. She took a steadying breath and firmly reined in her emotions.

He lifted his lips in an infuriatingly smug smile. "The point is that you want to kiss me as much as I want to kiss you. You no longer have a boyfriend and I no longer have a girlfriend. So what's the problem?"

She pondered her options. He was bluffing. There was no way Jay Nordstrom was attracted to her. For a fleeting moment Rachel longed to call the bluff and kiss that smug smile right off his face.

But before she could give in to the reckless impulse, the common sense she'd depended on since she'd been a child kicked in. "C'mon, Jay. Get real.

You don't want to kiss me anymore than I want to kiss you."

To her surprise, he didn't laugh and agree. Instead, he eyed her with an unblinking stare. "Are you saying I don't appeal to you?"

"Not in that way." Her tone came out calm and matter-of-fact and Rachel could have cheered. She'd sooner be boiled in oil than admit the truth.

"I've never really liked blondes," she continued, "and even if I did, we haven't known each other that long. While there are lots of women who don't think twice about kissing a man they barely know—"

"You're protesting again," Jay said, interrupting her nervous chatter.

"I am not pro—"

Jay leaned forward and splayed his hand against the table's edge, his eyes dark and intense. "Rachel, we're together every day. I've probably seen more of you in the past week than I saw of Lindsay in the entire six months we were together. We're far from strangers. Anyway, what's the big deal about a kiss? There's a lot of women out there who get more involved than that with someone they just met."

Though Rachel knew what Jay said was true, she'd never been okay with the casual intimacy so many of her peers embraced. If only these beautiful, talented young women would realize that God knew what He was doing when He said such intimacy should be reserved for the marriage bed. Making love should be something special, a physical and spiritual act between a husband and wife.

"Though you make a tempting case," Rachel said dryly, "I think I'll pass."

"I can see not getting more involved with someone you just met," Jay said, a curious gleam in his eye, "but not why you're making such a big deal about a little kiss."

Rachel shifted her gaze so he couldn't see the thoughts in her eyes. How could she tell him that she had the feeling that kissing him would be like eating a potato chip? It would be hard to stop at just one.

"Is it because of Tom?" he asked softly.

Rachel shrugged. If that's what he wanted to think, she'd let him.

Jay stared, his gaze thoughtful. "I'm surprised you broke up. You two seemed to have so much in common."

"We did," Rachel admitted. "We were in sync on all the important issues."

"Such as?"

"Our faith." A melancholy smile lifted Rachel's

lips. "After our second date, we attended church together every Sunday."

Jay choked on his milk. "Back when I knew Tom, you couldn't pry the guy out of bed before noon on the weekends. He'd laugh when I complained about having to be in church at eight."

"People change. Tom's not eighteen anymore. He knows what's important," Rachel said. "How about you?"

"How about me what?"

"Are you in church on Sunday morning?" she asked. "Or do you sleep in?"

"I'm in church on all the major holidays," Jay said immediately. "So I'm probably batting .250."

Rachel shook her head. It always amazed her how cavalier people could be about God and their faith. "Your life would be so much better, so much richer, if you'd just ask God to be a part of it."

He smiled as if she'd made a joke and reached for her hand. She jerked it back.

"Okay, don't get all bent out of shape." He raised his hands in a gesture of surrender. "I promise, one of these days, I'll send God an invitation asking Him into my life."

"I'm serious." Her irritation surged at his flippant tone.

"I'm serious, too." Jay's words were properly respectful but the twinkle in his eye gave him away. "I just hope that when I finally do invite Him, He doesn't choose an inopportune time to show up."

Rachel shook her head in disgust. How could you have a meaningful discussion with someone who refused to cooperate?

"I give up," she said. "It's obvious you don't want to talk about God."

"I'd much rather talk about you," Jay said matter-of-factly. He grabbed another cookie and sat back in his chair. "Tell me just what it is you're looking for in a man?"

Chapter Seven

What she was looking for in a man?

The comment, clearly designed to change the subject, caught Rachel off guard.

"Someone who shares my faith," she said automatically, giving him her number one criteria.

For a second she thought Jay groaned but then he smiled and Rachel decided she must have been mistaken.

"What else?" he asked.

"I'd like a man who wants to spend time with me," Rachel said, embarrassed by the admission, but not sure why. "I have lots of friends who are perfectly content being married to men who work eighty hours a week or travel three weeks out of four, but that wouldn't make me happy."

Jay nodded encouragingly.

"I want someone who is home every night so we can eat dinner together," she said, warming to the topic. "I want me—and our children—to be his priority."

"Tom met your criteria," Jay said.

"He did." For one brief moment in time, Rachel had been blissfully happy, convinced God had finally sent her the man of her dreams. "Although the bank kept Tom busy, he always made it a point to leave the office at six. That gave me time to get home from school and make supper before he stopped over."

"He expected you to have dinner waiting?" A hint of censure filled Jay's voice. "After teaching all day?"

"We went out sometimes." Rachel lifted her chin, wondering why, even now, she felt the need to defend Tom. "But I love to cook. You've lived alone. You know as well as I do that it's no fun cooking for one."

"I never cooked," Jay said. "I usually ate on the run. My lifestyle didn't leave much time for anything else."

"It sounds like work was pretty much your life," Rachel said.

Jay shrugged. "The only way you get to the top is by putting in the time."

"I can't imagine…" Rachel tilted her head. "Didn't you resent the long hours?"

"Not at all." A faraway look filled his eyes. "It never seemed like work to me. I can't even begin to describe what a thrill it is to be on the cutting edge of breaking news."

"I've watched a few of your broadcasts." Each time, Rachel had been impressed by Jay and his co-anchor's professionalism and camaraderie. "You do a great job. And there's a wonderful chemistry between you and Kathi."

"We had a good time," Jay said with a wistful smile. "She made work fun."

A fondness for his co-anchor was apparent in his tone. An unexpected pain stabbed Rachel's heart. "Did you and Kathi date?"

Jay laughed as if she'd made a joke. "I don't think her husband would approve."

"She's married?" Rachel couldn't hide her surprise.

"For almost five years," Jay said. "She and Rick had their first baby last year."

Rachel tilted her head and tried to imagine what it would be like to have a demanding career and a family, too. Just the thought of what you'd have to juggle boggled her mind. "When does she find time for her husband? Or her baby?"

Jay thought for a moment before he shrugged. "I

don't know. We never talk about that kind of stuff. All I know is they seem happy."

Rachel took a bite of cookie and chewed thoughtfully. "I'm not into a mother working when she has small children. That was another thing Tom and I agreed on."

"But you love teaching." Jay's voice rose in surprise. "And you're a good teacher with a lot to offer."

Rachel smiled at his biased support. "I like to think so."

"Why would you want to leave all that to stay home and change diapers?"

"Because other than God, my family will always come first in my life." Rachel eyed another cookie but didn't reach for it. "And I want a husband who sets those same priorities."

"Your parents both worked," Jay pointed out. "And you turned out okay."

"And your mother stayed home." Rachel leaned forward and rested her arms on the table. "Don't you see, it doesn't matter what our parents did. What matters is what *we* want out of life."

"But you need to be realistic. If your husband is the sole breadwinner, you can't expect him to put family first," Jay said. "If he doesn't focus on his career, he's not going to be successful."

"You mean he won't be able to give me the finer things in life?"

Jay nodded.

"But he will." Conviction flowed through Rachel's veins, strong and true. "By virtue of him being around for me and our children, he'll be giving me everything that matters."

Though he didn't call her on it, Rachel could see the doubt in Jay's blue eyes.

"I'm serious. I don't need a big house or a new car every year," Rachel continued. "I don't need to eat out every night or wear the latest fashions. I can be happy on less if I have what I really want."

"If you'd married Tom, you could have had it all," Jay mused. "The big house, new car *and* a husband home every night."

"Tom did seem to be everything I was looking for," Rachel admitted.

"What I can't figure out is why the two of you aren't still together," Jay said. "Is what's keeping you apart so big it can't be overcome?"

Rachel didn't answer. She just sighed as an all-too-familiar ache filled her heart.

"I think you should reconsider your decision to break it off," Jay said. "After all, where are you ever going to find anyone more perfect?"

* * *

Rachel pulled into her driveway that night and found Tom sitting on the front porch. Since he was dressed in a navy blue suit and crisp white shirt and tie, Rachel concluded he'd come straight from the bank.

His handsome face looked drawn and his stylishly cut hair needed a trim. The smile that used to linger on his lips was conspicuously absent.

Rachel's heart twisted. Other than those two times, Tom had been good to her and it broke her heart to see him so sad. Despite what Pastor Karelli had said, Rachel still wondered if some of this could have been her fault. After all, if it had never happened before…

"Rachel." Tom stood and dusted off his pants with the palm of his hand. "I hope you don't mind that I stopped by."

Though the curtains at the picture window across the street didn't so much as flutter, Rachel could feel Mrs. Kellogg's curious gaze. She wouldn't be surprised if her nosy neighbor had hidden a microphone in the tree so she could hear as well as see. But even if the woman didn't catch a word of conversation, Tom's mere presence on her porch guaranteed there would be talk.

It'll be all over town that Tom stopped by. Everyone will wonder if we're getting back together.

Rachel's heart clenched at the thought. It had been hard enough facing the questioning looks when they'd broken up the second time. His coming by tonight would only fuel the gossip mill and stir things up again.

"I don't want to be rude," Rachel said, "but I've made my feelings perfectly clear. I don't understand why you're here."

"There's something I need to tell you." Tom gestured with his head toward the front door. "Can I come in for a minute?"

Rachel folded her arms across her chest. "Why don't you just tell me here?"

His gaze darted in the direction of the house across the street. "I'd prefer we had this conversation in private."

Though she didn't want to give him any encouragement, Rachel couldn't help but smile. "She's probably already on her phone reporting your visit."

"Odds are we'll be the featured topic at garden club this week." Tom shook his head, a rueful smile lifting his lips. "Remember that time that I brought you home—"

"—and we caught her hiding in the bushes," Rachel finished the sentence and they both laughed.

"We've had some good times," Tom said.

Rachel's smile faded. "And some not-so-good ones."

He quickly sobered. "That was all my fault. If I—"

Rachel raised a hand. "There's no point in rehashing the past."

"There is a point." Tom must have seen the denial in her gaze because he continued without giving her a chance to speak. "Five minutes is all I need, Rachel. I promise, after five minutes if you want me to leave, I will."

Rachel's first impulse was to tell him to go now, yet a tiny voice inside her head reminded her that she'd recently given him three months of her life— surely she could spare a few moments to hear what was on his mind. She lifted a hand, fingers splayed. "Five minutes. That's all."

He nodded. "Agreed."

Tom held the screen while she unlocked the front door. She pushed it open and he followed her inside. Dropping her bag on the floor next to the living room sofa, she gestured to a chair.

"Aren't you going to offer me a soda?" Tom's lighthearted tone sounded forced.

"You won't be here long enough to drink it," Rachel said bluntly, determined not to be swayed by his charm.

"Good point." Tom smiled and took a seat.

Rachel sat on the corner of the couch, next to the chair. She fixed her gaze on him. "What did you want to tell me?"

He ran his tongue over his lips and nervously brushed a piece of lint from his sleeve. "I called Dr. Peters this morning."

Whatever Rachel had expected, it wasn't this. She lifted a brow. "Really? I thought you told me you didn't need anyone telling you what to do."

Tom raked a hand through his hair and the brief smile he shot her didn't quite reach his eyes. "I was a fool. Your telling me it was over hit me hard, Rach, real hard."

Rachel stared, the irony of the words not lost on her. "Funny, I thought it was you who hit me hard, Tom."

He opened his mouth to speak but she continued without missing a beat.

"And let's not forget the fact that you swore on your grandmother's Bible that you'd never do it again, but you did. Forgive me if I don't feel a lot of sympathy for how hard this has all been on you."

"I know," he said quickly. "I just meant that we had a good thing going and, given a little time, I could see it developing into something permanent. That's why when you told me we were finished, I knew I had to do something about my problem."

"I thought you said you didn't have a problem." Normally Rachel didn't like to play hardball, but she'd had it with excuses and empty promises.

"I realized I was wrong," Tom said. "That's why I called Dr. Peters and made an appointment. He'd had a last-minute cancellation and I went to see him today."

Tom had been so resistant to seeking help that the news that he'd actually seen a psychologist left Rachel momentarily speechless.

"You did?" she said, when she finally found her voice.

He nodded.

"What did he say?" Rachel asked.

"He thinks he can help me." Tom met her gaze. "And I told him I sure hope so, because my future happiness depends on it."

Before Rachel could ask him what he meant, he started talking. Only this time the words tumbled out, one right after the other, as if he were afraid she might interrupt before he could get them all out.

"I'm going to meet with him every week," Tom said. "And whatever he asks me to do, I will. But it would make such a difference to have your support while I work through this. After all, I'm not just doing this for me, I'm doing this for *us*."

"There is no more us," Rachel reminded him.

"There can be." Tom leaned forward and took her hand. "All you have to do is give me one more chance."

Chapter Eight

Once Tom left, Rachel paced the house, her mind a muddled mass of confusion. She'd meant it when she'd told him they were finished, but that was when he was still denying he had a problem and refusing to get help. Now, he'd actually taken that first step toward getting better. Could she turn her back on him?

If her mother were in town, she'd talk to her, but Mary had bronchitis and the baby was colicky. Her mother had her hands full.

After going round and round, Rachel ended up on the doorstep of one of her best friends. Dottie Douglas, a full-time mother to two-year-old Zach and the wife of the owner of the town's only hardware store, was sweet but capable of speaking her mind if she thought you were headed down the wrong path.

When Rachel had shown up on Dottie's doorstep, her friend had taken one look at her face, gestured for her to take a seat on the porch swing and disappeared into the kitchen. She'd returned with a large bag of chips and two sodas.

"I'm sorry to mess up your evening but I really needed to talk." Rachel smiled apologetically.

"Don't give it a second thought." Dottie waved a dismissive hand. "John works every Wednesday night and Zach is spending the week with his grandparents in Denver. Besides, having a friend over is a good excuse to bring out the snacks."

Rachel smiled and thanked God for wonderful friends.

Dottie held out the bag and jiggled it enticingly. "Want some?"

Rachel shook her head. Though the brand was her favorite, the way her stomach was churning, she didn't think she'd be able to keep them down.

Surprise flickered in the chunky brunette's eyes. The bag dropped to her lap. "This must be serious if you're turning down junk food."

"What would you say if I told you I'm considering getting back together with Tom?" Rachel blurted out.

Dottie froze, a chip suspended in midair. After a moment, she lowered her hand to her lap and visibly swallowed. Dottie shifted in her seat and the slats of the wooden swing creaked.

"I know how much you like him," Dottie said finally.

"But?"

"He hurt you, Rachel." Dottie's plump cheeks flushed bright pink. "And I'm afraid, given the opportunity, he'll hurt you again."

"He's getting help." Rachel surprised herself by rising to Tom's defense. "All he's asking is for a second chance."

"If I recall, he's already had that," Dottie said. "He promised you after that first time it would never happen again, but a month later it did."

"You're right," Rachel said, "but now he realizes he has a problem and needs help."

"Does he?" Dottie lifted a brow and turned in the swing to face Rachel, skepticism blanketing her face. "Or is this just a ploy to get you back?"

Rachel couldn't deny that same thought had crossed her mind, especially when she'd quizzed Tom about what he and the psychologist had talked about and Iowa football had seemed to be a main topic. Of course, she'd told herself, the counselor may have been just trying to put Tom at ease since it was the first time they'd met.

"I don't know, Dot." Rachel sighed and lifted her shoulders in a shrug. "He could be just playing games, but he seemed sincere. Do you know he got tears in his eyes when I told him I'd have to think about it?"

Dottie raised the chip to her mouth and bit into it with a loud crunch. "Of course he did. He knows you're the best thing that ever happened to him and he blew it."

"We were so good together," Rachel said softly. "He was everything I ever wanted in a man."

Dottie tilted her head and stared at Rachel as if she'd suddenly grown horns. "You wanted a man who hit you?"

Rachel could feel her face warm. "Of course not. I just meant—"

"That's the bottom line, Rachel," Dottie said. "I realize he's wealthy, but money doesn't buy happiness."

"Money has never been a factor." Rachel couldn't keep the indignation from her voice. Though she and Dottie had only grown close the last couple of years, she'd thought her friend knew her better than that.

"I'm not talking his family's fortune," Dottie said in a calming manner. "I'm just saying that being financially comfortable is part of what makes him so attractive. Since he doesn't really have to earn a living or build a career, he can afford to spend a lot of time with you."

Rachel flushed, realizing there was some truth in what Dottie said. Still…

"You make me sound like some pathetic, needy creature." Rachel couldn't keep the hurt from her voice. "Is that really what you think of me?"

"Of course not." Dottie's hand closed around Rachel's arm. "I only meant that it was easy for him to be the man you wanted."

"And what's wrong with that?"

"Nothing." Dottie shrugged. "I'm just not sure it's sincere."

A sick feeling filled the pit of Rachel's stomach.

"My mother used to say that actions speak louder than words," Dottie added.

"Are you saying Tom lies?"

"Well, we both know he lied to you about at least one thing."

Rachel pulled her brows together. "He did?"

"He said he'd never hit you again, didn't he?"

Chapter Nine

While driving to Bible study on Thursday night, Rachel couldn't help but remember the other times she'd been at Jocelyn and Adam Wingate's home. When she'd been dating Tom, the two couples had grilled out several times on the Wingate's large patio. Rachel had dreamed of one day doing similar family activities as Tom's wife.

Though Rachel had known it was probably not very Christianlike, she'd prayed on the way over that Tom would skip Bible study. She had a lot of hard thinking to do and she didn't want to see him until she'd made her decision.

But the minute she turned the corner, her heart sank. Tom's black BMW, freshly washed and waxed, sat in the driveway. For a moment, Rachel was tempted to drive on past.

After all, she hadn't missed Bible study in over a year and she went to church every week. Surely God would understand....

But as her car approached the front of the two-story house, she found herself easing the vehicle toward the curb. Shutting off the ignition, Rachel pocketed the keys.

Rachel had barely reached the front steps when the door swung open.

Pastor Tony stood in the doorway looking incredibly handsome and very unministerlike in a pair of khaki pants and a button-down shirt. "I thought I heard a car drive up."

His friendly smile enveloped her in its warmth, but Rachel sensed an undercurrent of concern when his gaze settled on her.

Rachel scanned the foyer. "Where's Jocelyn?"

"In the kitchen," Tony said, "frosting a *red* cake."

His dubious tone made Rachel smile, but she knew that it would only take one taste of the chocolate concoction for him to be a convert.

"I'll see if she needs help," Rachel said, but before she could take a step, Tony's hand closed around her forearm, stopping her.

"Tom's here," he said.

Rachel nodded. "I saw his car."

"How are things between you?"

Rachel wasn't sure what the minister was asking, but she answered honestly. "He told me he's started seeing a counselor. He wants us to get back together."

Tony's dark eyes met hers. "And what do you want?"

"I'm not sure," Rachel admitted. She was starting to wonder if she wanted marriage more than she wanted Tom, but she saw no need to tell the minister that. She'd already asked God for His guidance and some direction on the way she should go, but so far she hadn't gotten any sign. "I told him I needed some time."

Relief flickered across Tony's face.

Rachel frowned. "You look surprised. Did Tom say something different?"

Tony looped his arm companionably about her shoulders and lowered his voice. "He said the two of you were getting married."

"Married?" Rachel's voice rose. She hadn't even agreed to date him again, much less marry him. Still, she reminded herself that it was possible the minister had misunderstood. Perhaps Tom had merely said he *hoped* they'd be getting married.

"Hello, sweetheart." Tom stood in the doorway and smiled broadly. "I've told everyone the good news."

The smug smile on his face told her all she needed to know. Tony hadn't misunderstood. Tom had lied. Again.

Rachel reached behind her and opened the door leading outside. She smiled at the minister. "Could you tell everyone to just go ahead and start without us? Tom and I have something to discuss. Outside."

In her parents' home, her father had insisted that all the walls be white. The first thing Rachel had done after buying her tiny bungalow had been to paint every room a different color. For her bedroom, she'd chosen a soothing lavender that matched the threads running through her grandmother's quilt.

The tastefully decorated room was her refuge, a place where she could relax and let the cares of the day slip away. But tonight nothing could loosen the tightness in her shoulders.

She quickly changed her clothes and headed for the kitchen. Telling Tom that what they had was over had been surprisingly easy. The attempt to manipulate the situation had been the final straw and anger had fueled her words.

Rachel was glad they had been outside. Tom

hadn't taken it well. When he'd realized she was serious, the conversation had turned ugly. He'd accused her of everything from playing games to being frigid.

Somehow she'd managed to keep her cool, even going back into the house to say goodbye and clarify to her friends that there wasn't going to be any wedding.

On the drive home, it struck Rachel that she was going to miss the idea of having a husband and family of her own a whole lot more than she was going to miss Tom.

She opened the kitchen cupboard and pulled out a chamomile tea bag. In only minutes the water was hot and the tea steeping.

Where did I go wrong, God? Rachel cupped her hands around the mug and lifted her eyes heavenward. *Why can everyone else seem to find someone to love and I can't?*

Though Tom had a lot of wonderful qualities, he wasn't the man for her. Even if he could learn to control his anger, he was in many ways as controlling as her father. Trying to take the decision out of her hands by telling everyone they were getting married had told her that much.

And then when she'd confronted him, the words

he'd thrown at her had cut to the core. Frigid? He'd always said he supported her decision not to sleep with any man other than her husband. And to accuse her of playing games had been so off-the-wall she should have laughed. But the fact that she'd never really known him made her want to cry instead.

Her gaze drifted to the vase of spider mums and despair washed over her.

She was never going to be a wife. Never going to be a mother. Never going to have the kind of life she wanted.

Rachel took a sip of tea. It was still too hot, but she almost relished the scalding sensation against her tongue.

She brushed aside the self-pitying tears and lifted her chin. God obviously had other plans for her life. All she had to do was stay the course and have faith that He knew best.

She'd just picked up her Bible when the phone rang. Rachel sighed and set the Book aside, promising herself she'd read a few of her favorite passages before bedtime.

"Hello."

"Hello, honey."

Rachel recognized her mother's voice immediately. "What a pleasant surprise. I didn't expect to hear from you tonight. How's everything in K.C.? How are Mary and the baby?"

"They're fine," her mother said. "They're out at a church function. She and John asked me to go with them, but I thought it'd be best if they and the children went as a family."

Rachel's heart twisted. Though she was happy for her sister, she couldn't help feeling a little jealous. Mary had gotten it all: beauty, brains and a wonderful family.

"I'm happy everything is going so well."

"What's wrong, sweetheart?" Concern filled her mother's voice.

Although Rachel had done her best to project a cheery tone, she wasn't surprised her mother had been able to see through it. Her mother often knew what Rachel was feeling before she'd known it herself.

"Tom and I are through," she said.

"I knew that," her mother said. "You told me last week. Remember?"

"Yeah, well…" Rachel paused. "Tom started seeing a counselor. He asked for another chance but I said no."

"I can't believe he had the nerve…" Her mother's voice rose but she stopped, and when she spoke again her tone was soft and controlled. "You're better off without him."

"I don't think I'll ever get married," Rachel said with a heavy sigh.

"I know how much you liked Tom," her mother said when the silence lengthened.

Rachel thought back to the first time she'd met Tom. He'd pulled out all the stops trying to impress her and he'd succeeded. But he'd never made her heart beat fast. Not the way it did around Jay.

"What about Jay Nordstrom?" her mother asked, and for a second Rachel wondered if she'd spoken out loud.

"What about him?"

"He always seemed like a nice boy," her mother said. "You two are spending a lot of time together this summer. Maybe he can help take your mind off Tom."

"Jay's a good guy," Rachel said. "And we have fun together, but I'm not looking for another serious relationship right now."

"Is he?"

This time it was Rachel's turn to laugh. "Not at all."

"There you have it," her mother said. "You two are perfect for each other."

Chapter Ten

Henry had been gone about an hour when Jay heard the sound of Rachel's car in the driveway.

A few moments later her lilting voice drifted through the screen. "Pretty kitty."

Jay pushed himself up from the chair and hobbled over to the kitchen window, casting a curious glance outside.

Rachel stood bent over in the drive scratching the belly of Miss Kitty, his mother's favorite cat. Though the formerly skinny calico looked like it had gained a good ten pounds since his mother had left, Jay only had eyes for Rachel.

Her olive green shorts showed off her long slender legs to full advantage and the white T-shirt hinted at her soft curves. In the early morning glow, she looked fresh, wholesome and utterly appealing.

Jay moved from the kitchen to the front door, his slow deliberate steps at odds with the anticipation surging through his body.

The screen door opened just as Jay reached the foyer.

Rachel smiled when she saw him. "You're up early."

He returned her smile. "Did you get the movie?"

"They were all out of that one." Rachel dropped her overnight bag to the floor. "So I picked another I thought we'd both like."

Though Jay didn't really care what they watched, he'd had enough experience with women to know what that comment meant. "Does the plot of this other movie involve any dead bodies?"

Rachel shook her head.

"Any chase scenes?"

The corner of Rachel's lips twisted. "I don't think so."

Jay groaned. "It's a chick flick, isn't it? One of those syrupy boy-meets-girl, falls in love and gets married kind of movies."

Rachel shot him an innocent smile and headed

toward the kitchen, her silence telling Jay all he needed to know.

"I'll make the sacrifice." Jay offered up a melo-dramatic sigh and followed behind. "If you'll sit next to me on the couch."

Rachel stared at him for a long moment. "Okay."

"That's it?" Jay couldn't keep the surprise from his voice. For some reason he'd thought getting her to agree would be more difficult. "Just okay?"

"I'll be on one side." Rachel smiled and moved to the counter. "Lena will be on the other."

She dipped her head and hid her widening smile at his snort. "Where is she, by the way?"

Jay's great aunt was somewhat of an enigma—a petite woman, a recluse who shunned most people but never missed a church choir rehearsal…or bridge with her friends.

"She's still in bed," Jay said. "Her arthritis is act-ing up."

Rachel's hand stilled on the faucet. "Maybe I should check on her."

"She told me she was going to try to sleep a lit-tle longer."

"I'll take her a tray when breakfast is ready." Ra-chel began to make a pot of coffee with a quiet effi-ciency that still amazed him. His mother talked nonstop and her constant chatter grated on him, especially in the morning. Rachel never chattered or clanged pots and pans.

"Can I help?" he asked.

"I've got it under control." She turned and favored him with another smile. "I thought I'd make waffles. How does that sound?"

"Great." His mouth started to water just at the thought. "I'll set the table."

Surprise filled her blue eyes. "You don't have to help. Your mother is paying me to make your meals."

Actually, *he* was the one paying for her services, not his parents, but Jay saw no need to mention that fact.

"I want to do my share," he said. "Besides, one of these days, I'll be on my own again. I need to get used to doing this stuff for myself."

Rachel pulled some silverware from the drawer and handed it to him. She gestured with her head toward a cabinet built into the wall. "The placemats and napkins are in there."

Her comment made him smile. He'd set the table more times than he cared to count. Jay placed the forks and knives on the table and moved to the cabinet for the linens.

"Do the people you work with like living in Los Angeles?" Rachel tossed the question over her shoulder and poured a carafe full of water into the coffeemaker.

"Most of them." Jay grabbed the placemats from the drawer. "Otherwise they wouldn't be there."

Rachel turned around and rested her back against the counter. "What have you heard from Lindsay?"

Jay couldn't hide his surprise. Other than that first day, his ex-girlfriend's name hadn't come up. "Nothing," he said. "And I don't expect to."

"You don't think this is some kind of temporary falling out?"

"I hardly think so," Jay said with a grin. "It's been weeks since I've talked to her."

"What kind of woman do you think you'll marry?" Rachel pushed a button and started the coffeemaker.

The continuing stream of questions surprised Jay. Up until now Rachel hadn't seemed interested in him. Or his life. "I hadn't really thought about it."

"Yeah, right." Her tone was clearly skeptical.

"Probably someone in the industry," he said when he finally realized she expected an answer. "Someone who understands the pressures and demands of my job."

"But you don't have any special someone in mind now?"

"Look at me," he said bluntly. "Who'd want a guy who looked like this?"

"The right woman." Rachel pulled the waffle iron out from beneath the counter.

"If you say so," he said with a shrug. "Why all the questions?"

This time it was Rachel's turn to shrug. "No reason."

"Don't give me that," he said. "Something is on your mind."

Rachel kept her full attention on the batter she was stirring. "I just wanted to make sure you didn't have a girlfriend waiting in the wings."

Jay pulled his brows together. "What would it matter if I did?"

"Because I could never kiss someone who was involved." Rachel's blue eyes met his. "That's why I needed to make sure."

"You want to kiss *me*?" The look of startled surprise in Jay's eyes would have been laughable if Rachel hadn't been so appalled by her boldness.

"Not right now." She ignored the heat rising up her neck and concentrated on adding batter to the waffle iron.

"You told me you don't kiss casually," he said.

"Are you saying you think there could be something more between us?"

Rachel paused. Though she might not have a boyfriend anymore, she doubted there could ever be anything between her and Jay except friendship. But how could she say that without offending him? Especially after that crazy comment she'd made about kissing.

Apparently Jay mistook her hesitation for shyness, because the look in his eyes softened. "I've got to be honest, Rachel. I'm not the right guy for you. I don't—"

"Oh, for goodness sake." Rachel felt the warmth steal up her neck once again. "I'm not stupid. I realize that as much as you do."

Puzzlement filled his gaze. "Then what is this all about?"

"Tom and I are finished," she said.

"What does that have to do with me?" he asked.

"I just wanted you to know there's nothing between Tom and me. Not anymore." Rachel stumbled over the words, trying to figure out a way to explain. If her mother hadn't planted that insane idea of her being involved with Jay in her head, she never would have mentioned the kissing in the first place.

"You still haven't told me where I fit in?"

"I want us to be friends. I like you…as a friend."

Rachel lifted her chin and plunged ahead. "And, unless I've completely misread the signals you've been sending me, you like me, too. There's no reason we can't have fun this summer, is there?"

Jay lifted a brow, realization dawning in his eyes. "Would having fun include kissing?"

A shiver traveled up Rachel's spine. She smiled. "I guess anything is possible."

Rachel sat next to Jay on the couch and tried to focus on the romantic comedy rather than the handsome man at her side.

Jay chuckled and reached into the popcorn bowl.

He'd been a perfect gentleman all evening. Not once during the movie had he tried to steal as much as a single kiss.

But Rachel found it difficult to concentrate. Even dressed casually in khaki shorts and a cotton shirt, Jay looked like a *GQ* model. And he smelled heavenly.

The spicy scent of his expensive men's cologne teased her senses. She inhaled deeply and her heart fluttered.

It was crazy. She'd told him she just wanted to be his friend, yet now all she could think about was kissing him.

"Success at last." Jay nudged her with his elbow.

For the last half hour the couple in the romantic comedy had been thwarted every time they tried to be alone. It had gone on so long, she and Jay had joked that the two would probably remain apart for the whole show, but judging by the on-screen kiss, it appeared it was finally time for the couple to be together.

"Looks like fun," he added.

Though Rachel didn't turn her head, she could feel Jay's eyes on her and the heat rose in her cheeks. She kept her eyes on the screen.

When she didn't answer, Jay slipped an arm around her shoulder. "Want to try it?"

Rachel kept her gaze focused straight ahead and acted like she hadn't heard a word he'd said. Truth was, it was difficult to hear much of anything with her heart pounding like a bass drum in her ears.

Jay toyed with her hair. "Dad's gone all weekend and Lena is fast asleep."

Rachel resisted the sudden, overpowering urge to give in to temptation. He'd been so sweet, letting her have the popcorn pieces with the most butter and not saying a word when she'd opted for a soda rather than a beer. And he smelled so incredible. She moistened her lips with her tongue, removing a thin residue of salt.

Jay groaned. "Rach—"

The buzz of the doorbell stopped his words. For a second, Rachel thought the sound had come from the television, but a fist pounding on the front door ended that notion.

She frowned. "Who could that be?"

"I don't know," Jay said, looking equally perplexed.

The pounding intensified and Rachel stood. "I'll get it."

Jay placed a restraining on her arm. "Stay here. I'll get it."

He moved slowly, hampered by his cast.

"Open the door." The anger in the male voice carried through the thick oak. "I know you're in there."

"Oh, no." Rachel's hand rose to her throat.

Jay turned at the panic in her voice, his hand resting on the doorknob. "You know who this is?"

Rachel nodded, her eyes large in a suddenly pale face. "It's Tom."

Chapter Eleven

Rachel moved to the door and grasped Jay's arm. "Don't let him in. Not when he's acting crazy."

Jay stared at her for a long moment, a dawning look of understanding on his face. "You're scared of him."

Rachel nodded. She couldn't deny it. When Tom got like this, he did frighten her.

"Well, I'm not." Jay jerked the door open and moved protectively in front of Rachel.

Tom's gaze shifted from Jay to Rachel, then back to Jay.

"Tom." Jay smiled as if he was genuinely glad to see his old friend. "What a surprise. Come on in."

But Tom didn't return Jay's smile. Instead he fixed his eyes on Rachel, his lips pressed together in a hard line. "I went by your house but no one was home. Mrs. Kellogg said I'd probably find you here. Did I interrupt something?"

Despite the fact that nothing had happened, Rachel could feel a guilty warmth creep up her neck. "We were watching a movie."

"It's a chick flick," Jay offered with an easy smile, "but it's actually pretty good."

Tom's gaze settled briefly on Jay's casts before he glanced around the foyer. "Where's Henry?"

"Upstairs," Rachel said quickly before Jay could answer, hoping God would forgive her the little lie. "He wasn't feeling well so he went to bed early."

Though Jay might think he could handle Tom on his own, he was still recovering from his injuries. She hoped the thought that Henry was in the house would cause Tom to think twice about causing a scene.

Tom's gaze shifted from Rachel to Jay then back to Rachel.

"Now I understand why you weren't interested in giving me another chance." Tom's voice held a bitter edge.

"Why are you here, Tom?" Jay's tone remained affable. "Somehow I get the feeling it isn't because you wanted to reminisce about old times."

"She told me she didn't want anything more to

do with me." Tom's voice grew louder with each word and Rachel could tell by the look in his eye and the smell of beer on his breath that he'd been drinking. "I was in love with her. I wanted to marry her, but she threw my offer back in my face."

Though there was anger in Tom's voice, there was also pain and for one insane second Rachel found herself wanting to comfort him.

"I was nothing but good to her," Tom continued. "Treated her like a queen and she kicks me in the teeth."

Rachel stiffened. She stepped directly in front of Tom, her fists clenched at her side.

"Nothing but good?" Her laugh didn't contain even the slightest hint of humor. "You pushed me to the ground. You slammed my head against the wall and threatened to smash in my face."

Jay stilled beside her and though Rachel didn't glance his way, she could feel his eyes boring into her. "He did that to you?"

"Get out, Tom." Rachel lifted her chin. "And if you ever come near me again, I'm calling the cops."

"You heard the lady." Jay gestured with his head toward the door. "Get out."

Tom held up a hand. "Easy, buddy. We're old friends—"

"I don't have friends who hurt women." A hardness Rachel had never heard resounded in Jay's voice.

"You know women," Tom said, talking faster, his smile not reaching his eyes. "They make a big deal out of nothing."

Rachel gasped.

"You haven't changed, have you Tom?" Jay's voice was tightly controlled. "Just like with Karen, it was always her fault, not yours."

"Karen?" Rachel could barely get the name past her dry lips.

"He pushed her around." Disgust sounded in Jay's voice. He shifted his gaze back to Tom. "Is that why you two split up? Did Karen finally get sick of the abuse?"

Rachel stared, stunned. "You told me it had never happened before."

Her voice came out soft and shaky. She clamped her lips shut.

"He doesn't know what he's talking about." Tom took a step toward her but Jay stepped between them.

"I was there," Jay said. "I pulled you off her that time in the parking lot."

"I never hurt Karen," Tom protested.

"I suppose you were nothing but good to her, too?" Rachel met Tom's gaze.

"You need to leave." Jay gestured toward the door.

Irritation skittered across Tom's face. His eyes hardened. Rachel had seen that look before. Dread crept up her spine.

Tom's gaze settled on Jay. "You had something good going in L.A., but you screwed that up. The way you look you'll be lucky to get a job reporting hog futures."

Rachel gasped.

Jay's face turned white and his eyes glittered dangerously, but Tom had already turned back to Rachel. "And you—"

"Get out, Tom," Jay's voice was razor-edged. "Before I throw you out."

Tom glanced pointedly at Jay's casted arm and leg. "You really think you can do it?"

Jay took a step forward. "If you're standing here in five seconds you'll find out."

For the first time, Tom seemed to notice Jay's stiffened shoulders and steely-eyed gaze. He shrugged and turned on his heel. "You two deserve each other."

The minute he crossed the threshold, Rachel exhaled the breath she didn't realize she'd been holding and slammed the door. "Good riddance to bad rubbish."

Jay stared at her in surprise, then burst out laughing, the sound easing the tension in the air. "Where in the world did you hear that?"

"It's another of my mother's sayings." Rachel clutched her hands together to still their trembling. "You like it?"

"Very much." Jay laughed again. "And in this instance, it fits perfectly."

The encounter with Tom had left a bitter taste in Jay's mouth and he wanted nothing more than to head to his room where he could be alone with his thoughts. But, as his gaze settled over Rachel and he saw the look in her eyes, he knew that she needed him. Or at least she needed *someone* at her side right now.

He smiled. "How about we watch the rest of the movie?"

They resumed their seats on the couch and Jay hit the Play button on the remote before settling an arm companionably around her shoulders.

For the first time, he was grateful she'd picked a comedy rather than the thriller he'd wanted to see. They'd had enough drama tonight.

Though the movie was interesting, Jay's gaze kept drifting to Rachel. Her normally rosy complexion was pale in the dim light.

Anger surged within him at the thought of Tom

laying his hands on her. Rachel was a wonderful woman, so sweet and kind.

"I'm glad you're not with him anymore." The heartfelt words slipped past Jay's lips before he could stop them. Since she hadn't brought up the altercation with Tom, he wasn't sure she wanted to discuss it. He wasn't even sure *he* wanted to talk about it.

"Me, too," Rachel said softly. "He reminded me a lot of my father tonight."

"You deserve much better," Jay said fiercely, his voice shaking with emotion. "I can't believe he hurt you."

"I can't believe I let him," Rachel said with a chuckle devoid of humor. "I don't know why I didn't call it quits after that first incident."

Though her behavior might have surprised others, it didn't surprise Jay. He'd seen both sides of Tom and knew how persuasive the guy could be.

"I'm sure he said all the right things," Jay said, remembering how angry Karen had been and how Tom had convinced her to give him another chance. "He's a pro at stuff like that."

"I'm just glad I didn't marry him." Rachel lifted her face to him. "What would I have done then?"

"You would have left him," Jay said. "You would have gotten out. Just like Karen did."

Rachel's blue eyes were as clouded as a murky pond. "I never want to get a divorce."

"That's why you're not marrying Tom." Jay gave her shoulder a comforting squeeze. "You're going to wait until the right one comes along."

Rachel sighed. "Sometimes I wonder if there are any good men left."

"Of course there are," Jay said with more confidence than he felt. If he had a sister, he wouldn't let most of the men he knew near her. Or near Rachel. "And you'll find him. It may take a while, but it'll happen."

Rachel tilted her head. "You sound so sure."

"Trust me," Jay said, giving her a wink. "Good things come to those who wait."

Chapter Twelve

Jay waited until he heard the door to the den where Rachel was sleeping close before he headed to his room. Comforting Rachel had kept his mind from his own thoughts. But now that he was alone, they came flooding back.

What if Tom was right? What if he couldn't go back to network broadcasting?

Though his bedroom was relatively warm, Jay shivered. Being the best had been his goal since he'd been a little boy. He'd wanted to be successful before he'd even known what the word meant.

He moved across the bedroom to the window seat. Light from the moon illuminated the night sky. An owl hooted in the distance and the scent of honeysuckle filled the air. One deep breath was all it took for the memories to come rushing back.

He'd only been ten, and that night it had been the sound of raised voices that had pulled him from his bed....

"I'm not God." Henry Nordstrom's deep booming voice carried easily through the open upstairs window. "I can't make it rain."

"But if we don't get some moisture, we'll lose the crops." Despair filled his mother's voice. "We'll lose everything."

Fear gripped Jay's heart and he moved to the window, his breath coming in shallow puffs.

He might just be a kid, but he wasn't stupid. Jay knew what they were talking about—the farm, the land that had been in the Nordstrom family for five generations.

Crouching down so he wouldn't be seen, Jay peered out the window, his gaze sweeping the farmyard. His parents stood facing each other in the gravel drive. His mother's chest heaved as sobs racked her body.

Guilt formed a knot in Jay's stomach. Was this all because of him? After all, he *had* told God more than once how much he hated living in the country.

And he *had* begged God to find some way to let him move into town.

Somehow, though, Jay had never really thought about how this would all come about. He'd certainly never connected it with losing the farm. That was unthinkable. How could you lose something that had been in your family for over a hundred years?

"You never should have bought that combine." Accusation filled his mother's voice.

The combine had arrived three years before—on Jay's birthday. His father had teased Jay that the big green machine was one of his presents.

Jay had thought it was pretty cool since it had a CD player, but his mother hadn't liked it at all. After the party, she and his father had argued long into the night.

"How was I to know we'd have two years of severe drought? It hasn't been this bad in fifty years." Jay's father lifted his chin as if daring his wife to dispute his words.

"Okay, so maybe you couldn't have known." His mother's voice trembled with emotion. "But I'm tired of creditors calling and demanding money I don't have. Life isn't supposed to be like this."

Some of the changes that had occurred in the past six months suddenly made sense; his mother's desire to make their lunch rather than have them buy it at school, her learning to cut their hair and the decision to not run the air conditioner this summer.

"I'm doing the best I can, Twyla." Weariness filled his father's voice and it must have touched something within his mother because she moved closer, taking her husband's hands in hers.

"I know you are." Her words echoed in the still night. "I just hope it's enough."

It took all of Jay's willpower to stay silent. He wanted to scream at his father, to tell the tall broad-shouldered man he'd always admired that he agreed with his mother—it wasn't supposed to be like this. Fathers took care of their families.

Jay thought of the men in the co-op office asking him if he had something for them when he'd stopped by after school to grab a soda. He remembered the look they'd exchanged when he'd said no.

Warmth crept up his neck. Did his parents owe the co-op money? And what about the bank? Had that been what Tom had meant when he'd said Jay's father had begged his dad for help?

At the time, Jay had only laughed. He'd thought Tom was talking about help with harvesting and he knew his dad didn't need help from someone who owned a bank.

He wondered how he could have been so blind?

Jay had vowed then and there that he would never put his children in such a situation. He'd work hard. When he had a family, he'd provide for them. He'd never let them down.

A clap of thunder in the distance brought Jay back to the present with a jolt.

His finger moved to the scar on his cheek. What was it Tom had said? "You had something good going in L.A. but you sure screwed that up."

Though the crash had been ruled an accident, Jay knew it was his fault. He'd been driving too fast and now he was paying for his impulsiveness. Just like his father paid dearly for buying a combine he didn't need.

Most people in Millville thought of Jay's brother, Wayne, as a chip off the old block, but Jay knew that wasn't accurate. Wayne was a successful farmer.

He hadn't done one thing to screw up his life.

But Henry had.

And now, so had Jay.

The foldout sofa in the Nordstrom's downstairs den was relatively new but Rachel couldn't get comfortable. She tossed and turned for what seemed like hours.

Finally she gave up trying to fall asleep, pulled

a robe on over the boxer shorts and tank top she'd brought to sleep in, and headed for the kitchen. Hopefully some warm milk would do the trick.

She moved quietly. Even though Jay's room was upstairs, Rachel didn't want to take a chance on waking him. By the time the movie had concluded, exhaustion had been etched in Jay's features. And Rachel knew it was the altercation with Tom that had taken its toll, rather than Jay's increasing physical activity.

Jay had hidden his emotions well, but Tom's words had been a low blow, directed at the heart of Jay's fears. She'd wanted so much to tell Jay that even if he couldn't go back to a national network, he'd be able to do far better than a local station, but she'd kept still. Something told her that Jay might not find the sentiment comforting.

Besides, she was still reeling over the revelation that Tom had lied. Though Rachel felt sorry for Karen, the knowledge that she hadn't been the only one to experience Tom's abuse had been freeing.

Rachel padded down the stairs and across the hardwood floor to the kitchen. She'd just pulled the saucepan out from under the stove when she stilled, her brows pulling together. She listened intently for a moment, but only the ticking of the parlor clock greeted her ears.

HOW TO VALIDATE
YOUR
EDITOR'S FREE GIFT!
"THANK YOU"

1 Peel off the FREE GIFTS SEAL from front cover. Place it in the space provided at right. This automatically entitles you to receive two free books and an exciting surprise gift.

2 Send back this card and you'll get 2 Love Inspired® books. These books have a combined cover price of $9.98 in the U.S. and $11.98 in Canada, but they are yours to keep absolutely FREE!

3 There's no catch. You're under no obligation to buy anything. We charge nothing—ZERO—for your first shipment. And you don't have to make any minimum number of purchases—not even one!

4 We call this line Love Inspired because each month you'll receive books that are filled with joy, faith and traditional values. The stories will lift your spirits and gladden your heart! You'll like the convenience of getting them delivered to your home well before they are in stores. And you'll love our discount prices, too!

5 We hope that after receiving your free books you'll want to remain a subscriber. But the choice is yours—to continue or cancel, anytime at all! So why not take us up on our invitation, with no risk of any kind. You'll be glad you did!

6 And remember... just for validating your Editor's Free Gift Offer, we'll send you 2 books and a gift, *ABSOLUTELY FREE!*

YOURS FREE!

We'll send you a fabulous surprise gift absolutely FREE, simply for accepting our no-risk offer!

Order online at:
www.LoveInspiredBooks.com

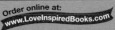

The Editor's "Thank You" Free Gifts Include:

● **Two inspirational romance books**
● **An exciting surprise gift**

YES!

PLACE
FREE GIFTS
SEAL
HERE

I have placed my Editor's "thank you" Free Gifts seal in the space provided above. Please send me the 2 FREE books and gift for which I qualify. I understand that I am under no obligation to purchase anything further, as explained on the opposite page.

313 IDL DZ3H   113 IDL DZ3G

FIRST NAME	LAST NAME

ADDRESS

APT.#	CITY

STATE/PROV.	ZIP/POSTAL CODE

Thank You!

▼ DETACH AND MAIL CARD TODAY!! ▼

(LI-EC-04) © 1997 STEEPLE HILL BOOKS

JOB 8

Steeple Hill Reader Service™ — Here's How It Works:

Accepting your 2 free books and gift places you under no obligation to buy anything. You may keep the books and gift and return the shipping statement marked "cancel." If you do not cancel, about a month later we will send you 4 additional books and bill you just $4.24 each in the U.S., or $4.74 each in Canada, plus 25¢ shipping & handling per book and applicable taxes if any.* That's the complete price, and — compared to cover prices of $4.99 each in the U.S. and $5.99 each in Canada — it's quite a bargain! You may cancel at any time, but if you choose to continue, every month we'll send you 4 more books, which you may either purchase at the discount price...or return to us and cancel your subscription.

*Terms and prices subject to change without notice. Sales tax applicable in N.Y.
Canadian residents will be charged applicable provincial taxes and GST.

If offer card is missing write to: Steeple Hill Reader Service, 3010 Walden Ave., P.O. Box 1867, Buffalo, NY 14240-1867

BUSINESS REPLY MAIL
FIRST-CLASS MAIL   PERMIT NO. 717-003   BUFFALO, NY

POSTAGE WILL BE PAID BY ADDRESSEE

STEEPLE HILL READER SERVICE
3010 WALDEN AVE
PO BOX 1867
BUFFALO NY 14240-9952

NO POSTAGE
NECESSARY
IF MAILED
IN THE
UNITED STATES

Rachel smiled and shook her head. No wonder she couldn't sleep. Obviously, her imagination had kicked into overdrive.

"Eeooww."

Startled, Rachel released her hold on the pan's handle. It fell to the stovetop with a clatter before toppling the rest of the way to the floor. It *was* a baby's cry and it sounded as if it was coming from the bathroom.

"Is something wrong?"

Rachel whirled. Jay stood in the doorway dressed in a pair of grey sweatpants and a T-shirt. His feet were bare and his brow was furrowed. Concern filled his gaze.

"It's a baby." She forced the words past her dry lips and brushed past him, panic propelling her steps.

"A baby?" Behind her Jay's voice rose and cracked. "What are you talking about?"

Rachel didn't take time to answer. She increased her pace and crossed the room in the time it would have taken her to answer.

The door to the bathroom stood ajar. The fact that Rachel could no longer hear the baby's cry caused her heart to tighten in her chest.

Though she wanted to burst in to the room, she carefully pushed the door open, her gaze darting around the small area. The sink was empty, as was the tub. Her gaze dropped to the floor.

"You heard the cat." Jay laughed, his voice drifting over her left shoulder.

The calico lay on the floor between the toilet and the wall.

Rachel's face warmed. What kind of idiot confuses a cat with a baby? She turned and met Jay's gaze. "I'm sorry I woke you. I tried to be quiet."

His lips twitched. "Was that before or after you dropped the pan?"

Rachel chuckled. "Point taken."

Jay gazed at her for a long moment, then raised one hand to cup her face.

Her breath caught in her throat at the look in his eyes.

"Have I told you lately how beautiful you are?"

Those brilliant blue eyes had viewed some of the most beautiful women in the world and Rachel knew she didn't hold a candle to those women. Still, she couldn't stop the flush of pleasure that filled her at his words. "With no makeup and bed-head? I don't think so."

"You're so oblivious." Tenderness mixed with wonder filled Jay's gaze. "You really have no idea how pretty you are."

Jay's fingers slid through her hair as he stepped forward. He stood so close Rachel could feel his heart beat, so close she could smell his clean masculine scent, so close she could scarcely breathe.

He was going to kiss her; she knew that with absolute certainty. And this time she was going to let him.

"Eeeeeeeowwww."

Rachel jumped back at the piecing cry, the sudden movement knocking Jay off balance.

He stumbled backward and would have fallen if Rachel hadn't sprung forward. She wrapped her arms tightly around him feeling his muscles tense between her touch.

"I'm sorr—"

"I'm not. I've got you just where I want you."

His arms tightened around her and anticipation crept up Rachel's spine. "And just where is that?"

He gently brushed back a strand of hair from her face. "In my arms."

She tilted her face to him and smiled. "In a bathroom?"

His smile widened. "Works for me."

"Even with a cat crying in the background?"

"I don't hear anything." Jay's breath was warm against her neck.

Rachel stifled a sigh and turned in his arms, over-whelmed by what she was feeling.

Jay pulled her close again, a satisfied smile lifting his lips. "It's great, isn't it?"

Rachel froze. "No, it's not."

"It's not?" At any other time the look of shock on his face would have been laughable, but the last thing Rachel felt like doing was laughing.

"Your cat is having kittens." She squirmed from his arms. "What are we going to do?"

By the time number five made her appearance, Rachel was exhausted. The births had not been easy and for the past hour she and Jay had had their hands full.

After each one was born, Rachel would give Miss Kitty a few moments to clean her baby off before handing it to Jay.

He'd positioned himself on the edge of the bathtub with a thick towel. With surprising gentleness he'd dry off each kitten before placing it in the tub in the nest of his mother's best Turkish bathsheets.

The calico had quickly joined her brood after the last kitten was delivered and the five little ones now lay cuddled up against their sleeping mother.

"They are so precious." Rachel reached down to

stroke the head of number three, a black-and-white female. "My father wouldn't allow pets in our home, so this is a first for me."

"It's a first for me, too," Jay said. "I've seen calves and pigs born, but never kittens."

Rachel had never lived in the country, but she knew that farm kids often had a different view of animals. Her dad had grown up on a farm and she remembered what he'd had to say on the subject. She'd been appalled when he'd told her the brutal way his parents had kept their cat population in check.

"My Dad said his parents used to drown their unwanted kittens in their pond." Rachel's gaze dropped to Miss Kitty and her sleeping babies. Somehow, after witnessing the miracle of life, her grandparents' actions seemed even more reprehensible. "And my father didn't think it was wrong. He said it made sense to him."

Jay's lips tightened. "I know he was your father, Rachel, but if he were here at this moment I'd be tempted to put him in a bag and drop him in the river."

"He wasn't a very nice man," Rachel agreed. She'd come to that realization years ago. "Thankfully I had a wonderful mother."

"Do you always look on the bright side?"

Something in his tone made Rachel glance up.

His expression was serious and the look in his eyes told Rachel he expected more than a flippant answer.

She wiped her hands slowly, giving the question some thought. "Though I have my moments of doubt, I'm an optimist. I prefer to focus on the good, rather than the bad."

"The good isn't that easy to find."

"It sometimes takes a little thought," Rachel conceded, "sometimes a little distance or time. But I can usually find the blessing in a situation."

The skeptical look in Jay's eyes told her he wasn't convinced.

"Think about it. My dad showed me by his example the kind of man I wouldn't want to marry," Rachel said. "All of his characteristics are red flags when I see them in someone I'm dating."

"And yet you dated Tom," Jay said. "And even considered marrying him."

Rachel could feel her cheeks warm. He wasn't saying anything she hadn't said to herself.

"Sometimes we miss what's right before us," she said finally, "but I can tell you I won't make that mistake again."

She expected Jay to smile, but his expression remained serious. "It makes me sick to think you were with a guy who treated you like that."

"My eyes have been opened," Rachel said, sending a prayer of thanks heavenward. "I now see Tom for who he is, and not who I wanted him to be. And I know I deserve better."

His handsome features relaxed and this time he smiled. "You go, girl."

Rachel rolled her eyes. "I might not know what the good Lord has in store for me, but I know now it's definitely not Tom Tidball."

"Trust in God and, in time, all will be revealed," Jay murmured.

Rachel widened her gaze. Just when she'd started to think she knew him, he surprised her. "Where did that come from?"

"I haven't a clue," Jay said, a hint of red creeping up his neck. "It's probably just those Sunday School lessons coming back to haunt me."

Rachel took a step forward and laid a reassuring hand on his arm. "Faith is a very attractive quality in a man."

He paused for a moment before his lips curved up and his arm reached out, pulling her close. "And in a woman."

Chapter Thirteen

Rachel hopped out of bed when the sun was barely peeping over the horizon. She pulled on a pair of running shorts and a T-shirt and headed to the washroom to check on the new arrivals.

She swore Miss Kitty smiled in satisfaction when she leaned over the bathtub and congratulated the feline on a job well done.

Since the kittens appeared to be in good hands, Rachel wandered into the kitchen, grabbed a glass of juice and headed to the back deck to watch the sunrise.

She must have dozed off because she opened her eyes to the sound of knuckles rapping on wood. She rubbed her eyes and blinked, trying to get her bearings.

"Rachel." Jay's impatient voice carried through the screen door. "Open up."

The urgency in his tone propelled Rachel from the chair.

"Hurry."

Was that pain in his voice? Rachel's heart picked up speed and her feet fairly flew across the decking. She jerked the door open wide.

"Good morning." Jay stood in the doorway with a broad smile on his face and a large tray in his hands.

Rachel couldn't believe he'd carried the heavy platter from the kitchen without losing his footing. The sterling silver tray held a plate of scrambled eggs and bacon, another plate of thickly buttered toast and two cups of steaming coffee.

Jay hesitated when Rachel moved forward to take it from him. "It's heavier than it looks."

"I think I can manage." Rachel smiled and carefully lifted it from his arms.

It *was* heavy. One misstep... Rachel cringed, thinking of him maneuvering across the slick linoleum floor.

"You could have broken your neck," Rachel said over her shoulder, placing the tray on the round wooden table next to her chair.

"First I'd have had to fall," Jay said with equanimity. "And I wasn't about to do that."

The smell of fresh coffee and hot bacon filled the air and Rachel's stomach growled.

Jay smiled. "Sounds like someone is ready to eat."

"It looks wonderful." Rachel filched a piece of bacon and popped it into her mouth. She chewed for a moment then swallowed. "And it tastes just as good."

Jay puffed with pride. "I'm glad you like it. Now sit down and prepare to be dazzled."

Rachel dropped the piece of toast she'd just picked up back on the plate. "I beg your pardon."

He gestured with his head to the chair. "Sit. I'm waiting on you this morning."

Rachel stared. None of this was making any sense. "But your parents are paying me to take care of *you*."

"Not this morning." Jay smiled. "Today is your turn to be waited on."

"Why? It's not my birthday or anything." But even as she spoke, Rachel gave in and sat down.

"Was that the last time you had someone wait on you?" Jay pulled out the chair next to her and took a seat. "On your birthday?"

Rachel popped another piece of bacon into her mouth.

"Actually *never* was the last time for me. I've lived alone for the last ten years and before that I was at home." Rachel took one bite of the eggs then promptly took another. "My father believed women should wait on men, not the other way around."

"My dad's the same way." Jay reached over, took one of the coffee cups from the tray and took a leisurely sip. "My mother insisted her sons be self-reliant."

His cooking expertise went far beyond self-reliant. The eggs, enhanced with Swiss cheese and chives, were scrambled to perfection and the bacon was just as she liked it—crisp without being burnt.

"It's a fabulous breakfast," Rachel said. "You're a natural in the kitchen."

"I like to cook." Jay smiled and relaxed against the chair, his fingers curved around the coffee cup. "I just never have time."

"Did you ever cook for Lindsay?" Rachel stabbed a piece of egg with her fork, finding the thought strangely unsettling.

Jay raised the cup to his lips and took a sip before answering. "Nope."

"Why not?" Rachel wasn't sure what madness

made her push the point. "You two were together almost six months. Surely you found time to cook once during that time."

"Lindsay was very social," Jay said matter-of-factly. "When we were together we usually went out."

"But what about when you spent the night?" Rachel asked.

"I never spent the night," Jay said. "Lindsay didn't like anyone to see her without makeup."

Did you sleep with her? For a second, Rachel thought she'd voiced the question niggling at her. But when he merely took another sip of coffee and stole a piece of her bacon, Rachel breathed a sigh of relief and rephrased the question. "Did you love her?"

Jay paused. His eyes took on a distant faraway look. Finally, when she'd given up hope of him answering, he shook his head.

"I like Lindsay a lot—" the fondness in his voice told her that much "—but no, I don't love her."

Rachel exhaled the breath she didn't realize she'd been holding. "Did she love you?"

Jay shrugged. "If she did, she has a funny way of showing it. I haven't seen or talked to her in weeks."

"You could call her."

It was as if someone else were talking, asking the ridiculous questions, pushing him back to a woman who hadn't cared enough to be there when he'd really needed her.

"I don't look back," Jay said simply, his gaze direct. "I've never seen the value in looking anywhere but straight ahead."

Rachel realized it wasn't just Lindsay he was talking about. This was his way of telling her that once he left Millville, he wouldn't be calling or making a special effort to keep in touch with her, either.

The food Rachel had consumed lay like a leaden weight in the pit of her stomach. She placed her fork on the tray and shoved it aside, knowing she couldn't eat another bite.

"Rachel?"

She sensed, rather than saw, the concern in Jay's eyes. "What's wrong?"

It wasn't until he touched her shoulder that she lifted her head and met his gaze.

"Once you go back to L.A.—I'll never see you again, will I?" Though she tried to keep her tone casual and offhand, anger and hurt resonated in her voice.

"Probably not," he said, his eyes never leaving her.

"I don't know why we couldn't remain friends." The word "friends" didn't begin to describe the feelings he stirred up inside her but it was the best she could do.

"Because I don't feel like your friend." His words came out on a sigh and he leaned his forehead against hers. "Not at all."

After a moment he took her hand and pulled her to her feet. "I worry about you."

Rachel raised her arms and wrapped them around his shoulders. She tilted her head questioningly. "Worry?"

"I don't like the idea of leaving you here with Tom." Jay's arm tightened protectively around her. "I don't want him bothering you."

"I'm afraid that's a given—" Rachel's lips quirked up in a humorless smile "—but I'm tough. I can handle him."

Tom had continued to call and Rachel had the feeling that wasn't going to stop anytime soon. And she had no doubt that once Jay left town, Tom's efforts would escalate.

"But if you and I were engaged, he'd leave you alone," Jay mused.

"Engaged?" Rachel could feel her eyebrows hit her hairline. "You want to marry me?"

"I want to protect you," he said. "Being engaged is a way I could do that without being here."

Rachel let out the breath she didn't realize she'd been holding. Her heart warmed, recognizing the caring behind the offer.

"I like you, Jay." Rachel whispered the words, though Aunt Lena was upstairs and there was no one else to hear. "So much."

Jay straightened and his eyes met hers, the show of emotion in his liquid depths taking her breath away. "With a face like this, I can't imagine why."

His chuckle didn't fool her. He was scared. Anger rose inside Rachel at the thought of his so-called "friends"—those who'd abandoned him, who'd said by their actions that he wasn't worthy unless he was perfect.

How could they not see the goodness in him? She remembered the strength he'd shown in standing up to Tom, the gentleness with which he'd handled each kitten and the kindness he'd shown her this morning.

Her gaze slid across Jay's face and the fact that there was still some redness and puffiness by his eye barely registered.

It was then that Rachel realized that she no longer saw Jay Nordstrom, the popular newscaster who'd once made the cover of *GQ,* but a friend, a man who in only a few short weeks had found a place in her heart.

Her heart swelled with emotion. Impulsively, Rachel leaned forward and gently kissed his battered cheek. "Any woman would be lucky to have you."

He pulled her to him and the world ceased to exist. The air seemed to carry an electrical charge and Rachel's heart fluttered wildly. In all her time with Tom he'd never had her in this state.

Rachel could feel Jay's breath on her neck and his hand against her shoulder. Warmth seeped through her shirt and into her skin.

After a long moment Jay lifted his head and tipped her face up to him.

His eyes were the color of slate and when his finger stroked her cheek, Rachel's heart thumped even faster. She held her breath as his mouth lowered to cover hers.

Rachel couldn't deny it anymore. She needed to find out what it was like to be held against him, to breathe him in and be thoroughly kissed. Just once.

His lips were warm and firm as they brushed against hers, then his mouth took possession. Rachel closed her eyes and gave in. It was nothing like she'd expected.

Jay stamped his mark on her mouth and her heart and she finally realized why she'd never lost her head with Tom. Because it had never been like this.

"What is going on here?" The horrified voice from the yard was like a splash of cold water.

Rachel's head jerked up. She gasped. Gladys Mitchell stood on the stairs to the deck, her eyes wide with shock.

Rachel suddenly felt naked and exposed. She straightened her shirt and moved to step away but Jay clamped a hand on her arm and fixed a steely-eyed gaze on the older woman.

"What are you doing here, Mrs. Mitchell?" Jay's tone was barely civil.

"Don't talk to me in that tone, young man," Gladys snapped. "Your mother would be horrified if she heard you talking to an elder in such a disrespectful manner."

A hint of a smile touched Jay's lips though his eyes remained hard and unyielding.

"My mother," he paused, giving the word extra emphasis, "would be horrified to learn you'd invaded her son's privacy."

"I knocked on the front door and rang the bell."

Gladys lifted her chin. "But when no one answered, I got worried and walked around the house."

If Rachel was feeling particularly generous she'd give the woman points for quick thinking. But she wasn't feeling generous. By the look on Jay's face, he wasn't, either.

"I don't think so," Jay said, his tone as hard and unyielding as his eyes. "I think you heard voices, wanted to snoop and seized the opportunity."

"If I wanted to snoop," the woman said, "I would have simply walked in the house."

Rachel had to concede that point. Most of the people in Millville and the surrounding county left their doors unlocked.

"You've been ill," Gladys continued unapologetically. "Like I said, I was worried."

"Well, as you can see, I'm perfectly fine."

The look in Gladys's eyes sent dread coursing up Rachel's spine.

"You two should be ashamed of yourselves." The woman's words may have been directed to Jay, but she'd shifted her attention to Rachel.

Rachel swallowed hard. "We were only kissing."

"Word is Henry is in Des Moines this weekend," Gladys said pointedly. "Leaving you two unchaparoned."

"I'm Jay's caretaker. And we're not alone. Lena is here." Though she was shaking inside, Rachel's voice sounded remarkably calm and matter-of-fact.

"Lena is a sweet woman, but I hardly think she's adequate supervision." Gladys's lips pursed together. "As evidenced by your shameless behavior this morning."

Rachel resisted the sudden overpowering urge to throttle the woman. "One little kiss like you'd give a friend."

The comment was meant to lighten the tension, but Gladys didn't even smile.

"It's time you leave." Steel edged Jay's tone. "What we do or don't do is none of your concern."

"None of my concern?" Gladys's voice rose and her gaze narrowed to tiny slits. "I'm a taxpayer in this county and that means I pay this woman's salary. She teaches my grandchildren. The kind of example she sets is very much my business."

The ramifications of what the woman was implying hit Rachel like a sledge. "You wouldn't."

"It's my duty," Gladys said.

Rachel jumped to her feet.

Jay's brows pulled together in confusion. "Duty to do what?"

"Report Miss Tanner's conduct to the school

board," Gladys said. "It'll be up to them to decide what action to take."

Rachel stepped back, her head spinning. Was her career over? The thought made her weak. She stumbled backward and might have fallen, but Jay reached out and placed a steadying hand around her waist.

Rachel knew she should pull away, but she didn't move and Jay's arm tightened around her.

"Tell me you're not talking about invoking some kind of moral clause," Jay said with a laugh. "Those went out at the turn of the last century."

"That may be true where you live now," Gladys said, clearly irritated by Jay's cavalier attitude, "but here in Millville we take such matters very seriously. Isn't that right, Rachel?"

"There isn't a morals clause in my contract." Rachel lifted her chin and forced the words past suddenly dry lips.

"Of course there isn't." Gladys gave Rachel a pitying glance. "Those liberals would take us to court over something like that, but we all know if a school district wants to get rid of someone, it will. Mrs. Peabody found that out."

Jane Peabody had been a nice woman, and a good teacher. Though Rachel would never condone adultery, she thought Jane had been treated too harshly, given the circumstance.

Jay frowned. "Who?"

"She taught junior high," Rachel said. "She was married. She had an affair with another teacher."

"Her contract wasn't renewed," Gladys added.

Disbelief flickered across Jay's face and Rachel could tell he'd finally made the connection. "Are you saying you could lose your job based on what this woman says?"

Gladys straightened, drawing herself up to her full five foot three inch stature. "I know what I saw."

Rachel thought of her classroom. Of the kindergarteners so sweet and innocent and so eager to learn. Her eyes filled with tears. Although she'd already signed her contract for next year, Gladys was right. If the board decided she had to go...

"Rachel?" Jay asked softly.

Rachel blinked back the tears she refused to let Gladys see and lifted a shoulder in a slight shrug. "Essentially she's right."

A muscle jumped in Jay's jaw, but otherwise he didn't react. A thoughtful look crossed his face.

Rachel wondered if he was considering apologizing. She hoped not.

He shot Rachel a slight smile and turned back to

the woman. "If you decide to run to the school board with your ridiculous tale, I hope you tell the whole story."

A tiny frown furrowed the older woman's brow. "I plan to be honest and tell them exactly what I saw—an unmarried teacher alone with a young man kissing, his hands—"

"Let me rephrase." Jay held up his hand silencing Gladys's protest. "You interrupted Miss Tanner kissing her injured fiancé. You—"

"Fiancé?" Gladys interrupted. "How can that be? Just last week Rachel was dating Tom Tid—"

"She was only *dating* Tom," Jay said firmly. "There's a big difference between dating and being engaged."

Gladys stared at him for a long moment, then her thin lips opened into a wide smile and her eyes took on an almost misty glow.

"I simply adore weddings." Gladys's hand rose to her bosom and she exhaled a sigh before her gaze shifted to Rachel. "Why didn't you say something sooner?"

Rachel smiled wanly, unable to utter a single word. But the funny thing was the older woman didn't seem to expect an answer.

Gladys clasped her hands together, her eyes fairly

dancing with excitement. "I can't believe I'm the first to know."

"It's usually customary to tell family first," Jay said pointedly.

Family?

Rachel had never fainted, but she wished she could now. Her world was spinning out of control and she didn't know how to stop it.

"I am so sorry I interrupted such a special moment," Gladys said, not sounding sorry at all. "I wish I could stay and chat, but I've really got to be going."

The octogenarian fairly twittered with excitement and when the woman started backing up, Rachel knew the news would be all over town by tonight.

Unless Rachel ended the madness right now.

Chapter Fourteen

"I should have said something," Rachel murmured. She stood next to Jay on the porch of the farmhouse, watching Gladys's four-door sedan spew gravel as it headed down the long drive to the highway. "I could have told her you were only kidding."

Only moments before she'd been about to do just that, but then Jay's lips had unexpectedly closed over hers. By the time she'd regained her composure, Gladys was already out the door and in her car.

Jay's eyes remained focused on the disappearing taillights, his fingers absently kneading the tension from her shoulder. "If you had, you'd have lost your job. And like we discussed, this way I can protect you."

The gentle massage seemed to be short-circuiting her brain. It took all Rachel's determination to stay focused on the conversation rather than on the sensations his fingers were evoking. "It was really all quite innocent."

Jay's expression sobered. "Innocent or not, Gladys would have trashed your reputation."

"And yours," Rachel said.

Jay waved a dismissive hand. Though he couldn't help but be touched, her concern was misplaced.

"We can't let people think we're engaged," Rachel said when he didn't respond.

"Why not?" Jay asked, meeting Rachel's gaze head-on. In the early morning light her eyes were as blue as the Iowa sky and her thick lashes the color of ripened wheat. She looked wholesome and pure and utterly appealing. "I did ask and you did say that any woman would be lucky to have me. Not to mention an engagement between us would take care of your problems with Tom."

Almost of its own volition, his gaze lowered to her lips and the memory of how it had felt to kiss her.

"I don't mind being engaged if you don't." Actually he rather liked the thought of being linked to Rachel, even if it was only for a couple of weeks.

"The problem is, once it ends, I have to live here

and deal with the aftermath," Rachel said. "You'll be back in L.A."

And in front of the cameras, God willing.

The half thought, half prayer arose from deep inside Jay, sucking the air from his lungs.

Next week he'd get the casts off. The way his face was healing, with the help of a little makeup, he could be back in the anchor chair by the end of the month.

If they still want me.

A chill traveled up his spine. They *had* to want him. That job was his life.

"Jay?"

Rachel's voice pulled him back and as he refocused he realized she'd continued to talk. "—I have to do it. I have to call Gladys and set the record straight."

Jay started shaking his head before she'd even finished. "Not a good idea," he said. "By the time you reach her she'll have already told at least fifty people. Besides, I'm not that bad of a guy, am I?"

Rachel shook her head and Jay's smile softened. "C'mon, babe. It'll all work out but only if we stay engaged for now."

"But—"

"And when we break up, I'll take the heat," he added. "I'll make sure you come out smelling like a rose."

If he'd thought that would pacify her, the look on her face quickly told him he'd failed miserably.

"No way." Rachel shook her head, her lips pressed tightly together. "I won't let you do that."

"I've already decided," Jay said in a matter-of-fact tone. "It only makes sense."

"To whom?" Rachel folded her arms across her chest and lifted her chin in a stubborn tilt. "I refuse to let you play the martyr."

Jay sighed. He'd come up against a brick wall and her name was Rachel. In a situation like this, there was only one solution. He shot her the smile that had been winning him hearts since grade school and…changed the subject. "We can work out the details later. Right now we have more important things to do."

"What could be more important than figuring out this mess?" Rachel asked.

"How about celebrating our engagement?" Jay said. "Since it's not going to last long, I figure we need to make every minute count."

"Fishing isn't what I had in mind when you said you wanted to celebrate." Rachel repositioned herself on the dusty bank of the Nordstrom's pond and wiped a bead of perspiration from her brow.

Though Rachel liked the outdoors as much as

anyone, by the time she and Jay had gotten the breakfast dishes cleaned up and Aunt Lena to her bridge group, the day was half gone, the sun was high overhead and the heat index was soaring.

"This is how everyone in L.A. celebrates their engagement," Jay said with a straight face.

Rachel chuckled. "I bet."

"And after a fishing expedition, they relax in a cabana next to the waterfront." Jay gestured to the red plaid blanket they'd spread out earlier in the shade of a tall cottonwood. "Care to join me?"

Rachel rolled her eyes. The guy had charm down to a science. And the crazy thing was she found herself wanting to play along. "If the deal comes with a cold glass of lemonade, count me in."

"That's my girl." Jay shot her a broad wink and took the pole from her hands. After reeling in the line, he placed it next to his on the bank and awkwardly pushed himself to his feet. Once upright, he appeared to sway.

Alarm raced through Rachel and she scrambled to her feet. It was only when her hands grasped Jay's arms to steady him that she discovered he didn't need any help. Hadn't needed any help. But when she started to release him, his hands moved to her waist.

Jay tugged her to him and Rachel found her arms rising and encircling his neck as if it were the most natural thing in the world. His eyes seemed to glitter, suddenly looking more green than blue in the bright sunlight.

She moistened her suddenly dry lips with the tip of her tongue. "What—?"

He reached forward with his right hand and pulled her chin up, then stopped her words by covering her mouth with his own.

The thought of pulling away didn't occur to Rachel. His lips were soft, warm and persuasive. She tightened her hold around his neck.

Rachel couldn't remember ever having been kissed quite like this before. It was a slow, leisurely sort of kiss, but one with a definite punch. It made her knees go weak. It made her tingle all the way to her toes. It made her wish it never had to end.

He released her unexpectedly and she stood there dazed in the bright sun. After a moment she found her balance and her voice.

"That was nice." She tried to sound blasé, but ruined the effect by sounding slightly breathless.

"It was more than nice."

The look in his eyes filled Rachel with womanly satisfaction. Apparently she wasn't the only one who'd been knocked off balance. Emboldened by the knowledge, she wrinkled her nose and batted her eyelashes. "Ya think?"

"I don't think. I know." He brushed his knuckles against her cheek. "It was fabulous. But then kissing is one of my many talents."

"I've never liked conceited men," Rachel said with a sniff, resisting the urge to smile and agree.

"You like me."

She tilted her head. "How can you be so sure?"

"Because," he said with a widening grin. "You told me once you never kiss men you don't like."

Jay stared up at the cottonwood leaves fluttering above him and sighed in contentment. Though he wanted nothing more than to pull Rachel into his arms, he remembered what had happened earlier and knew he'd be playing with fire.

While she'd been taking the picnic basket out of the truck, they'd kissed a few more times. But when Jay found himself wanting more, he'd brought the kissing to a halt.

Rachel was a woman with high moral standards, standards that Jay would never ask her to compromise.

He'd had to force the food past his lips, but Rachel hadn't seemed to notice. She'd chattered about the children who'd been in her classroom last year, telling him one amusing story after another until the heat, food and fatigue caught up with him. His eyelids started to droop.

He'd agreed to rest in the shade for a few minutes but only if she agreed to take a break, too. But her proximity drove all thoughts of sleep from his head and Jay found himself wide-awake.

"When I was a little girl we had a hammock in our backyard." Rachel's voice held a lazy edge. "I remember looking up at the sky when I was about eight—it was a cloudless day like this one—and wondering what I'd be doing in twenty years. Now, here I am, all these years later looking up at the same sky."

"When I was eight, just waiting for Christmas seemed like an eternity," Jay said. "Twenty years must have seemed like forever."

"I think that's why I picked it," Rachel said with a laugh. "It sounded like forever to me, too."

"Are you where you thought you'd be?" he asked, curious.

"I always wanted a little house," she said softly. "With each room painted a different color. I have that."

"You've also got a great career."

"And good friends," Rachel said.

"Appears to me you've got it all." Jay rolled to his

side and faced Rachel, propping his head up with one hand.

"Not quite," Rachel said. "But I have so much, it seems wrong to want more."

"What else is there?"

"Silly girl stuff," Rachel said. "You know—marriage and kids kind of things."

The hitch in her voice told him the importance of this "silly girl stuff."

"You'll have that, too," he said. "I know you will."

"I hope so."

He reached over, found her hand and gave it a reassuring squeeze.

To his surprise, Rachel didn't pull away. Instead she laced her fingers through his. "How about you?"

"What about me?"

"Do you want children?"

Jay paused. The truth was he'd never really given the matter much thought. He'd just assumed that someday he'd marry and have a couple of kids.

But did he *want* them? Jay thought for a moment.

"I'd like to have at least one child," he said finally. "More if my wife would agree."

Jay tried to picture Lindsay pregnant and the

scene just wouldn't compute. He couldn't imagine the svelte model ever letting her flat stomach swell into the size of a basketball. Besides, he wasn't sure she even liked kids. Lindsay wasn't the most nurturing of women. Not like Rachel.

Rachel would be thrilled at the thought of a new life growing inside her. He could easily picture her pregnant. And he could even picture the child she'd have: a tiny blue-eyed, blond-haired bundle.

The scene warmed Jay's heart until he realized that a blue-eyed blonde would only be guaranteed if she had *his* baby and that was never going to happen. Not because he wouldn't consider marrying *her*…but because Rachel would never consider marrying *him*.

Chapter Fifteen

"I didn't bring a suit with me," Jay said. "So this will have to do."

Rachel stared openmouthed. Jay stood in the foyer, wearing a dress shirt and tie, and a pair of khakis. Though the pants were tight against the cast on one leg and baggy on the other, he still looked wonderful.

As she'd gotten ready for church this morning she'd tried to be extra quiet. After all, if Jay stayed in bed while she was gone, she wouldn't have to worry about him falling. Since Lena was singing in the choir and needed to be at church early, her friend had already been by and picked her up.

Rachel felt guilty leaving Jay alone. But part of the deal she'd made when she'd agreed to stay for the weekend had been that she'd be gone a couple of hours Sunday morning. Jay hadn't balked, saying he usually slept in anyway. And now here he was at half past seven, fully dressed.

Jay smiled. "I'm going to church with you."

Rachel widened her eyes. "Why?"

"Why do most people go?" He lifted a brow, the innocent look on his face not fooling her in the least.

"You know what I mean," she said. "You never go to church. Why now?"

"My face is almost healed," he said. "It's time to make an appearance."

She'd gotten so used to seeing him that she barely noticed his injuries, but now that he'd mentioned it, she realized he was right. The discoloration around his eye had faded to the color of yellow putty and the swelling was almost gone.

Other than the casts, he looked more like someone recovering from a black eye than someone who'd had reconstructive surgery. It *was* time he got out. Still, he admitted he hadn't been much of a churchgoer in the past few years and it didn't make sense that he'd choose that venue to make his first public appearance. Especially when the diner would do just as well.

Of course, most of the town did show up for Sunday services and if he wanted to see everyone, that was the place to do it.

Rachel glanced down at her wrist. "We'd better get going or we'll be late."

She turned to the door, but a light touch on her arm stopped her.

"Wait," Jay said. "First you have to put this on."

She turned, her gaze immediately drawn to the ring resting in the palm of his outstretched hand. A curious tightness filled her throat.

"It was my grandmother's," Jay said hurriedly, not giving her a chance to comment. "She left it to me in her will."

It was a simple ring: a white gold band with an emerald cut diamond solitaire. The stone was a nice size—not too large, but not too small, either. It sparkled brightly, even in the foyer's subdued light.

Suddenly she understood why he'd gotten up early. "You didn't have to do this."

"I know," he said. "But you and I are in this together. We're a team. And that's the way I want the town to see us."

He smiled, slipped the ring on her finger and brushed a chaste kiss against her cheek.

It fit perfectly, and all the way into town Rachel was conscious of its weight upon her finger. She found herself wanting to glance down at it every few minutes, but after a couple of quick peeks, she quit looking, afraid Jay might notice and think she was making too much of the simple gesture.

But when she pulled in to the church parking lot and saw the cross at the top of the small clapboard structure, her doubts came flooding back. Could she really go inside and accept everyone's congratulations? Could she really show off her ring, knowing the engagement would soon be over? Could she really—?

"It'll be okay," Jay said softly. "I've got your back. Remember, we're a team."

Jay could see by the look in her eyes that she was scared. Heck, he was scared, too. This would be his first appearance in public since the accident. It had taken all his courage to make the decision to come and then follow through with it.

But lying in bed last night, he knew that he couldn't let her face everyone alone. And he couldn't let her go to church without a ring on her finger. In Millville, if you asked a woman to marry you, you'd better do the proposing with a ring in your pocket. He still remembered Wayne going to Des Moines to get the "perfect diamond" for Barb before he'd popped the question. If Rachel went to church without him *and* without a ring, everyone would talk. And this engagement was supposed to stop the talk, not fuel it.

By the time Rachel brought the vehicle to a complete stop and got out, there was a whole crowd of friends wanting to offer their congratulations.

No one seemed to notice his eye, or if they did, they didn't comment on it. Although a couple of guys he knew from high school did come over and kid him about his casts, calling him "hop-along," and try to push him off balance.

It was a great day to announce an engagement. The sun was warm on his face and the sky a brilliant robin's egg blue. Rachel had worn his favorite dress—a pink-and-white cotton that reminded him of spun sugar. He rested his hand against the small of her back as they entered the church, proud to be the man at her side.

They'd barely crossed the threshold when their progress came to an abrupt halt. Tom stood just inside the entry and Jay had the feeling it wasn't coincidental.

"Tom." Jay inclined his head slightly in greeting.

Tom's gaze flicked briefly over Jay and settled on Rachel. "Rumor has it you're engaged. That right?"

Though Jay could feel Rachel's back stiffen, she raised her chin and offered Tom a slight smile.

She didn't answer, but instead held up her hand, the diamond sparkling in the light.

"It looks old." Tom shifted his gaze to Jay. "You're smart not to spend a lot of money, considering you're out of work and Rachel could end up being the breadwinner in your family."

Jay's fist clenched at his side but he kept the smile on his face, refusing to let Tom know his words had hit their mark.

"Actually this ring was Jay's grandmother's. It has special meaning for both of us." Rachel, Jay thought, sounded surprisingly sincere.

"It's beautiful." Claire Karelli slipped in between Tom and Jay and gave Rachel a congratulatory hug. "Tony gave me his grandmother's ring, too."

"I remember," Rachel said. "It was at your birthday party shortly after you'd arrived in Millville."

"I wasn't sure I liked it at first," Claire said with a little laugh. "But I love it now. Of course, I still wouldn't turn down a box from Tiffany's—"

"What woman would?" The young minister came up and brushed a kiss on his beautiful wife's cheek. "By the way, where's our son?"

"Raye wanted to hold him for a while," Claire said. "You know my generous spirit…how could I refuse?"

Apparently satisfied that the baby was in safe hands, the minister turned his attention to Jay and Rachel. "I understand from Gladys that congratulations are in order."

Gladys poked her head around the pastor. "The news was just too good to keep to myself. I'm sure you understand."

Though he hid it well, Jay could see question and concern in Tony's eyes. The minister clearly had some reservations but was trying hard not to let them show.

"Rachel and I are engaged," Jay said. Impulsively, he reached down and grabbed Rachel's hand. "Rachel once told me God had a plan, that there was a reason I had the accident and ended up recuperating here. I know now, it was because she and I were destined to be together."

Tom snorted in disgust and walked off.

"Oh, my stars." Gladys's fingers rose to her lips and she exhaled a melodramatic sigh. "That is so romantic."

"What a sweet thing to say." Rachel stared up at him, a misty look in her eye.

Thankfully, Jay had never been the kind to blush, because if he had, he knew his face would be bright red by now. Once he'd started talking, he hadn't been able to quit. And where that last part came from, he didn't have a clue.

Some of the suspicion in Tony's eyes eased, and as Jay and Rachel walked into the church, the minister lowered his voice for Jay's ears only.

"Claire and I had a whirlwind courtship and marriage," Tony said. "I wish you the same happiness I've found."

Jay smiled and was thankful when the minister was waylaid by another parishioner so he didn't have to respond.

"Is this okay?" Rachel pointed to the back row. "I usually like to sit further down, but see how this pew jogs over? You can stretch out your leg."

"Looks good to me."

He settled into the hard wooden pew and after the first hymn Jay realized with a start that, since he'd arrived at the church, not one person had said anything about his face.

"I think I must be looking better," he whispered to Rachel. "No one has commented on my appearance."

"That's what I've been trying to tell you," Rachel said. "You look fine. Besides, these people are on your side. They're pulling for you."

All through the sermon Jay considered her words. He thought about his friends in L.A., friends who'd been too busy to help when he'd gotten out of the hospital, friends who'd been too busy to call since he'd been in Millville.

Rachel was right. The people in this town were his friends. Other than Tom, of course. And Gladys.

Jay smiled, picturing the woman running all over town spreading the news.

"What's so funny?" Rachel tugged on his sleeve, her low whisper pulling him back to the present.

"Nothing," Jay said in an equally low tone, breathing in the light floral scent she was wearing today and finding it very much to his liking. "I'm just happy to be back among the living."

"Happy to be back in church?"

"Happy to be in church sitting next to the prettiest girl in town," Jay said, jostling her arm with his elbow.

An older couple in the next pew turned around and smiled and Jay realized he'd forgotten to speak softly.

Red crept up Rachel's neck.

"Sing," Rachel hissed, shoving a hymnal into his hands.

Suddenly lighthearted, Jay grinned, took the book and began to sing.

* * *

"Engaged?" Henry shook his head. "I've never heard anything so crazy."

"Tell me what you really think," Jay said with a wry smile.

Though his father had offered his congratulations to both of them when they'd told him the news this afternoon, Jay knew his father would never have let on if he'd been displeased, not with Rachel standing right there.

Rachel had headed home after dinner, blushing when Jay had insisted on giving her a kiss goodbye even though his father was in the room. Now it was just the two of them. Jay briefly considered telling his father how the engagement had happened to be, but decided the way he'd become engaged didn't really matter.

"You're moving mighty fast," Henry said, pulling his cigar box from the cabinet in the living room. "Still, I think you've got yourself a good woman."

His father's words sent a flush of pleasure coursing through Jay. "Rachel is the best."

"Cigar?" Henry held out the box.

This time it didn't occur to Jay to refuse.

"Sure," Jay said. "After all, we need to celebrate."

They sat there puffing contently for several minutes, talking about his father's weekend in Des Moines and the busy week he faced in the fields.

And as they talked, Jay realized that the wall that had stood between them for as long as he could remember no longer seemed quite so formidable.

"When's the wedding?" Henry asked, blowing a smoke ring in the air.

"We haven't even talked about a wedding." Jay placed his cigar in the sauce dish. "The decision to become engaged was a spur of the moment thing."

"Spur of the moment or not, she'll make a good wife. But there's nothing wrong with a long engagement. I assume she'll be going back with you to L.A.?" Henry asked in a conversational tone.

Jay stifled a groan. Just when he thought they had this whole mess covered, something unexpected popped out of the woodwork.

"She'll be staying here," Jay said. It would be disastrous if someone got the notion Rachel wanted out of her teaching contract.

"Staying here?" His father's voice rose and he sat up straight in the weathered easy chair. "Why in the world would she be staying here?"

"Her job is here." The explanation made complete sense to Jay, but the minute the words left his mouth he knew he'd said the wrong thing. His father was old school—no commuter marriages or separate anything for him.

"Her place is with her husband," Henry said.

"We're not married yet," Jay said in as reasonable a tone as he could muster. "Only engaged. And we don't think it's right to live together."

Henry nodded approvingly. "It won't be easy for the two of you to be so far apart."

His speculative gaze settled on Jay.

"I'll miss her, that's for sure." This time Jay didn't have to pretend. The emotion behind the words was all too real.

An understanding smile lifted Henry's lips. "I'd like to tell you that after thirty years it gets easier being apart from the one you love, but it doesn't."

His father's words surprised Jay. He'd never really thought of his parents as being in love.

"When I was younger, you and Mom fought so much there were times I thought you might split up."

"We went through some hard years," Henry said. "But we'd made a commitment to each other, a solemn vow before God, just like the one you'll make with Rachel. One way or the other, you stick together and make it work."

"What if you can't?" Jay asked, thinking of all the guys he knew with one or two failed marriages already behind them. "What if you wake up one morning and discover the love is gone?"

"Love can return," his father said quietly. "If that ever happens, you pray and ask God to show you the way back together."

"But—"

"With God nothing is impossible," Henry said with the assurance of a man who'd seen God's power in his own life.

"You know that's just what Tony said in his sermon this morning," Jay said.

"Son—" Henry hesitated.

Jay lifted a brow.

"You and Rachel are going to have your share of troubles." A hint of red crept up Henry's neck. "All married folks do. Don't ever be afraid to ask the Lord for His help."

"I won't." Jay hoped he wouldn't have to ask God's help, but the way things were going he might need it. He had the uneasy feeling that ending this engagement might not be as easy as he'd first thought.

Chapter Sixteen

Rachel had just finished pulling on her pajamas when the phone rang. "Hello."

"How's my favorite fiancée?"

The sound of Jay's voice sent a ripple of awareness up Rachel's spine and she smiled into the phone.

"I'm just getting ready to hop into bed." Rachel plopped down on the sofa and tucked one leg beneath her. "My mother kept me on the phone until just a few minutes ago or I'd be there now."

"Your mother?" Silence filled the phone line for several seconds. "Did you tell her about the engagement?"

Rachel swallowed hard, remembering her mother's reaction. "I told her."

"What did she say?"

"She was concerned things were moving too fast." Rachel sighed. "What is it about being engaged that suddenly makes everyone an expert on marriage?"

"I know what you mean," Jay said. "I couldn't shut my dad up."

"He's not happy, either?" Rachel's voice couldn't hide her disappointment. She'd always thought Henry liked her.

"Happy?" Jay laughed. "The guy is positively ecstatic."

The tenseness in Rachel's shoulders eased and her lips relaxed into a smile. She knew it was stupid—given the fact that she and Jay weren't really getting married—but she couldn't help but be glad Henry approved.

"Unlike your mother," Jay added.

"She's just a worrier," Rachel said, hoping he wasn't getting the wrong idea. "She had a bad experience with my dad. But she's glad I'm not with Tom."

"Rachel—" Jay stopped, paused, then started again. "I don't want you to be hurt by any of this. The point of this whole charade is so you wouldn't be hurt."

"I won't be," Rachel said. "I know the score."

After reassuring Jay for several moments, Rachel hung up the phone and sighed. She really was going to miss the guy.

"I'll be wearing long sleeved shirts and pants the rest of the summer," Jay announced over lunch the following Friday.

Rachel took a sip of iced tea and tried to hide her smile. The doctor had taken both of Jay's casts off that morning and he'd been shocked at the scaly pale skin beneath the cast.

Personally, Rachel didn't think it looked that bad.

"A little lotion and a few days out in the sun will work wonders," Rachel said. "At lest you can walk without limping. And the doctor said that fracture in your arm couldn't have healed any better."

Jay smiled. "I'm almost good as new."

"Can I get you anything else?"

Rachel swore the college-aged waitress had stopped by the table every five minutes since they'd sat down. Other than actually writing down her phone number and telling him to call, the brunette had let him know in every way possible that she was interested and available.

Jay hadn't seemed to notice. He'd been polite to the coed, but distant.

"We're fine." Rachel smiled and brushed her

hair back with her left hand, making sure the girl saw the ring.

On their way out of the restaurant, Rachel couldn't resist teasing Jay. "The waitress wrote down her name and number. She wants you to call."

"Throw it out." He sounded disgusted. "If I'd have wanted her number, I'd have asked for it."

Rachel realized with a start that he didn't know she was kidding. Apparently women *did* give him their phone numbers and ask him to call. And often enough that it didn't even surprise him.

But before she could set him straight, his arm settled companionably around her shoulders and she forgot everything except how good it felt to be next to him.

In the past week, Rachel had learned that Jay was a very demonstrative guy. And she'd discovered something about herself, as well. Though she'd never been into public displays of affection, she found she liked it when Jay held her hand or took her arm. She'd grown accustomed to being kissed goodbye at night and welcomed with a hug and kiss every morning.

Henry only smiled and chuckled at his son's behavior, telling Rachel once when they were alone that he was glad to see his son finally in love.

Of course, Rachel knew Jay wasn't in love, but

merely acting for her sake. Still, having never been engaged before, Rachel found herself enjoying the experience.

"Want to walk around the mall?" Jay asked. "I'd like to stretch my legs before getting back into the car."

Rachel put a finger to her lips and pretended to think.

"Hmm. I'm a woman and you're asking me if I want to hang out in the mall." She shook her head. "Naw, I'd rather head back to Millville."

Jay laughed out loud. He reached up and tugged on a piece of hair. "Brat."

"I'm serious." Rachel knew she'd be more convincing if she could just keep her lips from twitching.

"And I'm serious, too." He pulled her close. "About this."

Jay's mouth closed over hers and Rachel melted against him, raising her hands to his shoulders, then around his neck. Though they stood in the middle of a busy outdoor mall, Rachel didn't rush and neither did he.

She put all the emotions that had been churning inside her into the kiss, and when they finally reluctantly separated, her insides trembled.

"Wow." Jay raked his fingers through his hair. "I wish I'd done that sooner."

"Jay." Rachel ran her fingers lightly up his bare arm, and his muscles tensed beneath her touch. "We don't have much time left together. So, anytime you want to kiss me, you go right ahead and do it."

Jay smiled. "Anytime?"

Rachel thought for a moment. Would there be a time when she wouldn't want Jay to kiss her?

No, she thought, but there would be a time when Jay wouldn't be around.

"That's right," she said. "Anytime."

Rachel unlocked the door to the Millville Elementary School and turned to Jay. "Are you sure you don't mind doing this?"

"I volunteered, remember?" Jay held the door open and gestured for her to go first, then followed. Once inside, his gaze rose to take in the old building's vaulted ceiling. "Besides, I haven't been in this place since I was a kid. This gives me a chance to look around."

They walked down the wide hallway side by side. The brown-and-black floor tiles gleamed like polished satin beneath their feet.

"It still smells the same." Jay stopped and inhaled deeply. "Funny how a scent can bring back memories."

Rachel smiled in understanding. Even after all

these years, she could stand in the halls, close her eyes and be transported back twenty years. "Were you a little boy who liked school?"

Jay looped an arm around her shoulders and leaned close. "Let's just say I would have liked it a whole lot better if I'd had a pretty teacher like you."

His breath was warm against her ear and a shiver traveled up her spine. When he pulled her to him, she let the bag of artwork drop to the floor and slipped her arms around his neck.

"I'm not sure I should let you kiss me. After all, we are on school property." Even as she said the words, Rachel wove her fingers through his hair and lifted her face to his, anticipating the feel of his mouth against hers.

"What are you going to do?" he teased. "Send me to the principal's office?"

His hair was like spun silk against her fingers.

"Maybe," she said impishly.

A hint of smile lifted his lips for an instant, then disappeared. "I'm not going to kiss you."

Rachel's head jerked up and she blinked in confusion, a wave of disappointment washing over her. "You're not?"

Jay shook his head and the smile returned. "*You,* Miss Tanner, are going to kiss *me.*"

Rachel pulled her brows together and tried to force a stern look, but instead she found herself laughing out loud, the sound echoing in the cavernous halls.

"Rachel." He took a step closer.

They were few inches apart. When her eyes lifted and met his, the connection between them was almost palpable.

His eyes were remarkably beautiful. As Rachel looked into them, at the flecks of gold and green that adorned the blue, his gaze flickered for a moment, down to her mouth.

It was just a second, maybe two, but the message was clear. He wanted to kiss her just as much as she wanted to kiss him.

She rose on her tiptoes and brushed his lips with hers. But when she started to back away, he pulled her close. By the time his mouth left hers, Rachel felt dazed.

"We should get to the classroom." Rachel ran a shaky hand through her hair and forced a bright smile. "There's lots of work to do when we get through here—I still need to bake a pie before the party tonight."

They walked in silence down the hall, her knees a little weak from the spark between them.

How had she lived so long without experiencing

this? This was what had been missing with Tom. It was this tingle, this connection that had been absent. She hadn't felt any of this when Tom smiled at her. Her insides hadn't melted, her heart didn't beat harder—

The way it did when Jay kissed her.

It wasn't logical and it certainly didn't make sense.

Jay was a summer romance, not a lifetime love. His life was going in one direction, hers in another. There was no way he could be the one God intended her to be with for the next fifty years.

Despite all that, she was in love with him.

And somehow that made the least sense of all.

Jay placed his glass of iced tea on the end table in the living room. Rachel had chased him from the kitchen, telling him she'd call when lunch was ready. He'd taken the not-so-subtle hint as her polite way of saying she didn't need an extra set of hands.

Not like this morning. He'd spent several hours helping her get the classroom ready for the next batch of first graders. Though she technically didn't need to report for duty for over a month, she'd gotten word the painting in her building had been completed and she couldn't wait to get "things back in place."

His duties had been relatively easy. He'd helped

her move furniture and held cut-outs up while she'd eyed them for spacing. He'd even hung a paper "tree" that went all the way from the floor to the ceiling. Though Jay wasn't sure what "R blend" words were, she'd assured him that first graders loved to put examples of those words on the tree.

The awkwardness between them had eased as they'd worked side by side. She'd started talking and just by listening to her excited chatter, he'd learned a lot about the Millville curriculum and about her. When he'd picked up a book about an ugly badger who'd been teased by the other animals, tears had come to her eyes. With a little prompting she'd told him about one of her pupils, a sweet little boy named Timmy who suffered from a rare genetic disorder that affected his appearance. At this point, his classmates were supportive, but she worried that could change as he got older.

He still remembered the surprise that had filled her gaze when he'd asked what she'd do if that was her child. *Why, love him with my whole heart* had been her reply.

Jay leaned back in the living room chair, sipped his iced tea and reflected on her words.

There were a lot of pressures in today's society.

It was easy to get caught up in all the superficiality. A child would be lucky to have a mother like Rachel.

A man would be lucky to have Rachel as his wife.

The telephone's ring jarred him from his thoughts.

"I'll get it," Jay called out. He grabbed the receiver. "Nordstrom residence."

"Jay? Hugh Thompson."

Jay's fingers tightened around the receiver. Hugh was from the network. The one who'd told him dispassionately when he was getting ready to go in for reconstructive surgery that it was too soon to say if there would be a job for him when he was ready to return. He was also the one Jay had left a message for two days ago, letting him know he was ready to face the cameras again.

Until now, he hadn't heard so much as a peep from Hugh. And, though Jay had tried, he hadn't been able to convince himself that no news was good news.

"Hugh, thanks for calling me back." Jay made sure his voice came out casual and offhand. There was no use letting Hugh think he had the upper hand…even if he did.

"I'd have gotten back to you sooner but there were a few things I had to check out first."

Jay's heart clenched at the man's serious tone, but then he reminded himself that this was Hugh, a guy who didn't have a lighthearted bone in his body.

"I'm ready to get back into that anchor chair." Jay made a conscious effort not to sound overly eager.

"That's what you said." Hugh paused.

"I could be there August first," Jay added, in case Hugh hadn't listened to the whole message or had forgotten.

Silence filled the phone line.

"I'm afraid that's not going to work," Hugh said at last.

Beads of sweat broke out on Jay's brow and for a second he felt almost light-headed.

Dear God, they don't want me back.

Breathe, he told himself, just breathe.

Though Jay wanted nothing more than to demand an answer, desperation wasn't the image he wanted to present. So he took a couple of steadying breaths, sat back in the chair and waited for Hugh to tell him if he had a future at the network or not.

Chapter Seventeen

"Your fiancée makes a great pie." Tony stabbed the last forkful of sour cream–peach from his plate.

Jay sipped his drink and smiled. He'd already had two pieces of the pie Rachel had brought and if it weren't all gone, he'd have a third. "My parents used to have card parties but I never remembered them doing a pie exchange."

Rachel had explained the concept to him when she was rolling out the crust. Each woman attending Dottie's party would bring a different kind of pie. After the couples were through playing cards, everyone would be encouraged to try a variety of pies.

Rachel had baked her contribution in his kitchen. When the smell of warm peaches had filled the farmhouse, Jay had known right away the one he wanted to sample.

He smiled, remembering how she'd slapped at his hand when he'd tried to sneak a taste while it was cooling. Of course he'd turned the tables, capturing her hand and bringing it to his lips.

As if mere longing had conjured her up, Rachel appeared and it seemed so natural to slip his arm around her waist and pull her close. A sense of rightness flowed through him. He'd enjoyed hanging out with the guys tonight, but she was the one he wanted at his side.

Rachel smiled. "How's it going?"

"Good," Jay said. "Tony and I have been getting acquainted."

At the beginning of the evening, Jay had known Tony only through his sermons, but as the night had progressed, they'd had plenty of opportunity to talk and Jay had discovered the minister had a sense of humor in sync with his own.

"So everything is okay?" A hint of worry laced Rachel's tone and Jay knew the questioning look in her eye was because he'd been on his own most of the night. From the moment they'd walked through the front door of Dottie and John's home, the men had congregated in the living room while the women had gathered in the kitchen.

Even when they'd played a board game, Jay hadn't been with Rachel. They'd been paired with the opposite sex but he'd been "assigned" to Rachel's friend, Jocelyn. Though Jocelyn was fun and certainly beautiful, he'd missed Rachel.

All evening his gaze had sought Rachel out. Her pale blue sleeveless dress was demure, but she'd worn her hair loose like he liked it and when she stood beside him, as she did now, the fragrant scent of the perfume he'd bought her on their shopping trip to Des Moines tantalized his senses.

"I'm having a great time," Jay said. The casual affair was a far cry from the elaborate network parties he'd attended, but it had been a nice change of pace.

Some of the tension seemed to leave Rachel's face. "Thanks for being such a good sport."

"Thanks for inviting me." Jay leaned over and impulsively brushed a kiss across her brow.

"Rachel," Dottie's voice rose above the conversational din. "We're waiting."

Rachel shot him an apologetic look. "There's a quilt she wants—"

"Don't explain," Jay said. "Go."

"She's obviously worried about the company

you've been keeping this evening," Tony said with a grin as Rachel hurried off.

"Hanging out with a minister is definitely a first for me." Jay smiled. "And to make it worse, you're not even a local."

Tony lifted both hands. "Guilty as charged."

"Where *are* you from anyway?" Jay asked.

"My father was in government service and we lived all over the world," Tony said. "But if I had to pick a place to call home, it would be D.C."

"I can't believe you moved here." Jay shook his head. "D.C. has so much to offer while Millville…well, let's just say my hometown isn't exactly a cultural center."

"It has culture," Tony said with mock seriousness. "The Jazz in July ice cream social featured six flavors of ice cream along with the high school combo."

Jay chuckled and took a sip of his drink.

"Seriously, the adjustment wasn't as hard as I thought it would be." Tony's expression turned thoughtful. "Both Claire and I were ready for something different. Only a few years before, we'd have laughed if you'd told us we'd end up in a small town in the middle of Iowa. But we like it here. And I truly believe it's where God wants us to be. What about you?"

"Me?"

"Have you and Rachel discussed where you'll live after you're married?" The minister's tone was nonchalant, but concern filled his gaze.

"My job is in Los Angeles," Jay said, knowing that didn't answer the question, but hoping Tony would let it go at that.

"Rachel's job is here," Tony pointed out.

"She can teach anywhere," Jay said.

Tony took a sip of coffee and lifted a brow but he didn't comment. "Is she excited about the move?"

Jay took his time answering and chose his words carefully.

"She thinks L.A. is too big," Jay said. "But she's never been there or seen where I live. I've got a great condo that I know she'd like."

"I'm sure you're right," Tony said. "But it will probably still take her a while to adjust."

Jay's gaze slid across the room to where Rachel stood talking animatedly to Dottie and a couple of other women. The diamond ring on her finger flashed brightly. Though he knew it was impolite to stare, he couldn't look away.

How had he ever thought it would be easy to leave her behind?

"I assume Rachel will stay here until after the wedding?" Tony asked.

"That's the plan." Jay sighed. "I just never realized how hard it was going to be to leave her."

Tony patted him on the shoulder, an understanding smile on his lips. "Spoken like a true man in love."

In love?

Jay was tempted to dismiss the sentiment. After all, he'd said he'd miss her, not that he loved her. Still, he had to admit that his feelings for Rachel had deepened in the last few weeks. Every morning he looked forward to her arrival and every night he hated to see her leave.

His relationship with Rachel went far beyond mere fun and games. They talked about issues and feelings.

Just recently she'd opened up and told him how she'd always felt like an ugly duckling next to her sister. He'd reciprocated and confessed his fear of being cast aside like last year's news when he was no longer good enough or attractive enough to be in the spotlight. Sitting on that porch swing, comforting and being comforted, he'd never felt so close, so connected to another human being.

Tony was right.

He did love Rachel.

Now he just had to figure out what he was going to do about it.

"I feel like I've hardly seen Jay all evening." Rachel rinsed a couple of pie plates and handed them to Dottie to put in the dishwasher.

Over the years Rachel had attended enough of these events to know you rarely saw your date. That fact had never bothered her. Until tonight.

The way Jay's eye was healing, she figured they only had another week or two left. Then he'd be gone.

I'll never see him again.

The realization brought a stabbing ache to her heart. Even if he came back for holidays it wouldn't be the same. That's why she was determined to spend every waking moment with Jay. That's why it was driving her crazy to spend the evening talking to people she could talk with anytime.

"He seems to fit right in." Dottie took a plate from Rachel's hand. "I'm going to hate it when you get married and move away. It'd be such fun if you were in town and the four of us could get together."

"Maybe Jay could get a job around here." Rachel found herself voicing the hope that had lingered on the edge of her conscious thought all week.

"And maybe I'll get a job as a model in Hollywood." Dottie laughed and patted her rounded hips. Though her friend's words were flippant, Dottie's eyes were filled with understanding. "I know how hard it is to leave your home and go somewhere new. I hated leaving Denver, but when John's father took sick and wanted him to take over the business…"

Rachel just nodded. Dottie thought she understood. After all, she'd relocated for her husband. But Dottie had grown up in a town the size of Millville and had always liked small-town life. Rachel had experienced life in a large city and she'd hated everything about it—the crowds, the traffic and the anonymity. And even if she could get past all that, with such a demanding career, Jay would be gone more than he'd be home.

Rachel wouldn't be happy in that environment. Not even if she was with the man she loved.

"I love Jay." The words popped out of Rachel's mouth before she could stop them.

"Of course you do." Dottie giggled. "You wouldn't have agreed to marry the guy if you didn't love him."

But Rachel hadn't agreed to marry Jay. It was just a charade, a joke.

But this joke had ended up being on her.

Because she'd gone and done the unthinkable.

She'd fallen in love with her fiancé.

* * *

"I'm glad you suggested walking home from the party," Rachel said.

Stars filled the night sky with tiny pinpricks of light while the moon cast a golden glow, lighting their way down the darkened streets. The air was warm and only a light breeze ruffled Rachel's hair. Though it was barely past midnight, most of the houses were silent and dark and it was as if she and Jay were alone in the world.

Rachel sighed in contentment. She couldn't imagine anything better than this.

"The evening went so fast," Jay said. "But then this whole week has flown by."

She wished he hadn't mentioned time. She was trying to ignore the big clock ticking in the back of her head, counting down the hours and the minutes until he'd be gone.

"I overheard you on the phone this morning," she said, surprising herself by the admission. "Sounds like they want you back."

Rachel had been in the kitchen when he'd taken the call in the living room. She'd been on her way to tell him lunch was ready and had heard him talking. Though she'd known it was wrong to listen in, she hadn't been able to stop herself. The excitement in his voice and his responses told her it had been about his job.

He'd been in a great mood the rest of the day, but he hadn't said a word. She'd told herself that she wouldn't mention it, she'd let him bring it up. But now in the comforting cloak of darkness, she couldn't wait any longer.

"They definitely want me back."

Rachel could hear the relief in his voice and see the glow in his eyes. Though her heart sank, she forced a smile. "I'm happy for you."

"At first I wasn't sure it was a go, but apparently the guy who replaced me didn't click with the viewers," Jay said. "Ratings are down."

Rachel thought back to the times she'd watched Jay and his co-anchor. There had been some indefinable chemistry between the two that had been almost palpable. "Is Kathi worried?"

Jay shrugged. "Probably. I'm sure she's hoping my return will help the ratings slump. If not, we could both be out of a job."

"Out?" Rachel didn't even try to hide her surprise.

"You're only as good as your ratings," Jay said matter-of-factly, though she guessed he was nowhere near as blasé as he appeared. "That's why I need to get back."

"How soon?" Rachel wasn't sure how the question made it past the sudden lump in her throat.

"I was hoping to hold off until the first but they need me right away."

"How soon?" Rachel repeated.

"My flight is scheduled for Friday," he said. "I wanted to tell you earlier but I didn't want to spoil the evening."

"This is Saturday." Rachel refused to give in to the almost overwhelming urge to count off the days remaining, knowing it would only be more upsetting if she put a number to her fear.

But she didn't need to count to know this would be their last Saturday night together. Never again would they gather with friends as a couple. Never again would he kiss her and call her his fiancée. Never again would she be so happy and content.

Her ring finger dipped with the weight of the ring she would soon give back as her gaze settled on the man she loved.

Was it possible for a heart to break in two? At this moment, it seemed highly likely.

Dear God, why did You bring this man into my life only to take him from me?

"This is our last weekend together."

"It doesn't have to be." Jay turned to face her, his

hands gripping her arms, his expression solemn and intense. "Come with me to Los Angeles, Rachel. I can't bear the thought of leaving you behind."

Chapter Eighteen

Rachel stared at Jay, a stunned expression blanketing her face. "Go with you?"

The words came out as a husky croak and Jay smiled. He took her hands in his. "I want you to marry me."

"For real?"

Jay grinned at the surprise in her voice. "Of course for real. I love you."

Though it was dark outside, they were close enough to a streetlight that Jay could see a shadow cross Rachel's face. "The engagement isn't real."

His heart softened at the wary look in her eyes.

"It will be," he said, pulling her to him. "All you have to do is say yes."

"Oh, Jay." Rachel laid her head on his chest and he could feel her heart fluttering in her chest.

He wished she'd answer, wished she'd accept his proposal, wished she'd put an end to his misery. But the longer she remained silent, the more his sense of unease grew.

"I love you so much."

At first Jay thought he'd only imagined the words, until she lifted her head and her eyes met his. Then it was all there for him to see.

"You do?" he stammered.

Her lips curved up in a smile and she nodded.

At that moment she reminded him of an angel: her golden hair glistening like a halo, her ivory skin flawless in the moon's glow and the light of love shining in her eyes. His heart overflowed with emotion.

"We're going to be so happy." The words spilled from his lips one after the other as joy rose inside him. He'd been worried for nothing. "You'll love L.A. I know it's big, but it's not as intimidating once you get to know—"

"Wait." Rachel pushed back from his chest and shook her head as if clearing her thoughts. "What was I thinking? I can't move to L.A."

For a second, Jay froze, then he realized of course

she was talking about her house and everything she'd have to get ready before a move.

"It doesn't have to be right this minute." Jay brushed back a strand of hair from her face with the tips of his fingers. "I have almost a week before I have to leave. That should be enough time for you to get things together. Of course, there's nothing that says you couldn't take an extra week or two. I'd miss you but I'd—"

"Jay."

He'd been babbling, he realized. Because in her eyes he saw something he didn't want to see and he was afraid if he quit talking he'd hear something he didn't want to hear.

"You have to understand," Rachel said softly. "After I left Chicago I swore I'd never live in a big city again."

"But you were alone," Jay said, trying not to overreact. "It's hard to be in a strange place, especially one with millions of people, and not know anyone. But in L.A. you'd be with me and you'd already have a circle of friends to build on."

"I don't know." Though her words were worrisome, the indecision in her eyes gave him hope. "You'd be gone so much."

Jay found himself tempted to lie, to reassure her

that he'd be home every night, but he couldn't do it. He'd always been honest with her and wasn't about to start their future married life with a lie.

"My job keeps me busy," he admitted. "I can't say it doesn't. But it's not like I'm at the studio 24/7. We'll have lots of time together."

A dog barked his agreement from a nearby backyard.

"See," Jay said. "He agrees with me."

"We'd better start walking. Or old man Krupicka will be out in a flash."

The dog barked again and Rachel grabbed Jay's hand and tugged him down the sidewalk. He glanced over his shoulder at the small bungalow. "Are you sure he's still alive?"

Rachel smiled. "He still cuts meat three days a week. Not much changes here. That's why I like it."

"Change isn't bad," Jay said, reassured by the feel of her hand in his. "We met each other and that was a change, but a good one."

She squeezed his hand but remained silent.

He wanted to press her for an answer to his proposal but he kept his mouth shut, reminding himself that Rachel wasn't like most women. She thought things out. Spontaneity was foreign to her. Her head and heart worked hand in hand.

After two blocks, Jay could stand the silence no longer.

"Tell me what you're thinking," he said.

"I was thinking about my parents," Rachel said after a long moment. "They weren't a good match and because of that they had an unhappy life together. If my dad hadn't been killed in that car accident, I think they would have ended up getting a divorce."

"What made you think of them?" Jay made a conscious effort to keep his voice casual and offhand.

"I don't want that kind of life," she said with a sigh. "I want the fairy tale, a happy-ever-after kind of life. It's what I've always wanted."

His hand tightened around hers, but he made himself keep walking.

"You can have that with me," he said. "Guaranteed."

"But we're so different." He could hear the regret in her tone. "What we want out of life is so different."

"I don't agree," Jay said. "We both want to work at a job that makes us happy. We want to socialize with friends. We want children."

"What about God?" Rachel asked. "Where does He fit into the picture?"

"I have to admit that in the last few years, God

hasn't really been a part of my life," Jay said honestly. "But I do believe. And if we had children, I'd want them to go to church. When I wasn't working, I'd go, too."

"Oh, Jay." Rachel's face twisted in disappointment and his heart sank.

"Oh, Jay, what?" he asked lightly, trying to bring the smile back to her lips.

"I know what I want out of life and what will make me happy," Rachel said. "I want to live in a small town. I want a husband who works a regular schedule, who is home at night. And most of all I want to marry someone whose faith is as important to them as mine is to me."

"I thought marriage was about compromise," Jay said.

"Some things are non-negotiable."

"So you're saying, I'm not the man for you." Jay's heart hardened protectively against a fresh surge of pain.

"I wish you were, but you're not." Rachel sighed. "It's no one's fault. It's just how it is. You are such a wonderful man. Any woman would be luc—"

"Spare me," Jay said. He was a big boy. He didn't need her to sugarcoat the rejection. "Bottom line is you're turning down my proposal."

Rachel slowed to a stop on the sidewalk in front of her house. "I am."

As angry and hurt as Jay was, the sadness reflected in Rachel's eyes made him want to forget his own pain, pull her into his arms and comfort her. He kept his arms at his side.

"Where do we go from here?" Jay asked, knowing he needed to ask, but wasn't sure he really wanted to hear the answer.

Rachel's gaze shifted to her left hand. "I need to give you back the ring."

Though accepting it graciously would probably be the sensible thing to do, taking the diamond back made it all seem so final. Besides, the reason it was on her finger hadn't changed.

"Keep it," he said. "At least for now. It would look suspicious if we broke up so soon."

She thought for a moment, then nodded. "You're right."

"Of course I'm right," Jay forced a light tone. "I'm always right. And, I can tell you, Miss Tanner, one of these days you're going to look back and regret turning down my proposal."

"You think so?" Rachel asked, a ghost of a smile touching her lips at his teasing tone.

"I know so," Jay said. "I'm a great guy. And I could have made you very happy if you'd just given me a chance."

If you'd just given me a chance.

Rachel stared up at her bedroom ceiling, wishing desperately she could fall asleep, but knowing there was no chance until she sorted through the thoughts swirling in her head.

When Jay had told her he loved her, she'd been filled with joy. Though she'd tried to temper the emotion with logic, for one crazy moment she'd found herself believing that it *could* all work out.

But when he'd started talking about L.A. and how much she was going to like it, reality had reared its ugly head and she'd returned to her senses.

As a child, she'd turned up her stereo to drown out the sounds of her parent's fighting. She remembered growing up in a home with tension so thick you could cut it with a knife. She remembered vowing that she would never subject *her* children to such turmoil.

When she married, she would choose carefully, knowing the choice of a spouse was the most important decision she would ever make.

But I want Jay.

The cry rose up from deep inside Rachel, bringing tears to her eyes and deepening the ache in her heart. Though she'd once fancied herself in love with Tom, her feelings for Jay went so far beyond what she'd felt for Tom that she couldn't begin to compare the two.

Jay had opened up and let her see the man inside the hunky body. It hadn't been easy for him, and Rachel had the feeling that most of his past relationships had been fairly superficial.

He'd soon be back in L.A. Who would keep him grounded? Who would comfort him when he was stressed? Who would be a true friend?

Lindsay?

The tabloids had reported Lindsay and her latest boyfriend, a scruffy looking rock star, had just split, so she was available. And with Jay back to being his old handsome self, she'd certainly find him an acceptable companion.

But Jay needed someone who loved him for who he was, not what he looked like—someone who understood him, not someone like Lindsay who couldn't even be there when he needed her.

Rachel folded her hands and lifted her eyes heavenward.

Dear God, I know this may seem like a trivial request, but I know You love Jay and want what's best for him. This is an uncertain time for him and I don't want him to make any mistakes. Lindsay Stark may be a nice woman, but she's not the right woman for him. You know as well as I do that Jay's faith needs to be bolstered and raised up, not torn down. I know he comes across as supremely confident, but You and I both know the fears in his heart. Let him feel Your comfort and strength. Surround him with those who truly care. Thank You. Amen.

Rachel closed her eyes, suddenly at peace. Jay would be okay. Even if she were no longer the one watching over him.

Rachel closed the hymnal and sat down along with the rest of the congregation. She folded her hands for the final prayer and wondered if she should have called Jay this morning instead of assuming the plan hadn't changed. Earlier in the week, when he'd mentioned picking her up for Sunday services, she'd told him she had to come early for an Altar Guild meeting so she'd just meet him at the church.

But that had been before she'd turned down his proposal. Her heart twisted. Saying no had been the hardest thing she'd ever done, but it was the only decision that made any sense. A marriage between her and Jay would never work.

"Amen," the congregation intoned in one voice.

Rachel lifted her head and realized with a guilty flush that she hadn't heard a single word of the prayer.

The organist launched into the final hymn and Rachel sang with extra gusto hoping God would know by her enthusiasm that He was still first in her heart, even if her thoughts had been a bit preoccupied.

The song ended, the blessing was given and Rachel rose along with the rest of the parishioners. After exchanging pleasantries with one of her sister's former classmates, Rachel headed up the aisle.

She'd barely taken five steps when a hand grabbed her arm and pulled her to the side. Rachel turned and discovered the steel-fingered grip belonged to Gladys Mitchell.

Rachel forced a smile and rubbed her arm. "For a second I thought I was being hijacked."

"We missed you at Altar Guild," Rachel added when Gladys didn't immediately reply.

"My alarm clock misfired." Gladys's smile faded and she shook her head in disgust. "My nephew gave it to me for my birthday last week. It's one of those newfangled machines that are supposed to do it all. I just wanted it to wake me up on time. I guess that was too much to ask."

Rachel started to laugh, then covered it with a

cough. "Rae took notes. She said she'd give you the schedule for next quarter."

The older woman's lips pressed together. "If that alarm had gone off, I'd have been there to take my own notes."

"Maybe it didn't like the early hour," Rachel quipped, knowing she probably shouldn't tease Gladys, but was unable to resist.

"It's not early to me. But then I go to bed at a decent hour," Gladys said with extra emphasis. "I hear you were out late last night."

"Not so late." Rachel ignored the censure in Gladys's tone. "Dottie's party broke up around eleven."

"I was referring to your late-night stroll through town."

Rachel widened her eyes. "How did you hear about that?"

Gladys gestured toward the front entrance where Elmer Krupicka and a group of men stood talking. "There aren't many secrets in Millville."

Rachel laughed. Truer words were never spoken.

The older woman's gaze darted around the sanctuary. "By the way, where is that handsome fiancé of yours? I don't think I've seen him this morning."

Somehow, Rachel managed to keep the smile on

her face. "I'm not sure. We were supposed to meet here."

Though the evening hadn't ended on a particularly high note, she'd never thought Jay would stand her up.

Gladys's gaze narrowed. "Did you two have a spat?"

Rachel could feel warmth creep up her neck. She shook her head. "No."

"Where is he then?" Gladys demanded.

"I don't know." To Rachel's dismay a tiny hitch sounded in her voice. She prayed Gladys hadn't noticed.

"He probably has one of those clock radios like mine," Gladys said, her tone surprisingly reassuring. "Probably works just as well, too."

Rachel wondered if it could be that simple. Had Jay merely overslept?

"Henry wasn't here, either," Rachel said, almost to herself. "And he rarely misses church."

"Give 'em a call," Gladys urged. "It's nearly noon. Those two should be up and going by now. You can use the telephone in the church office."

"I've got my cell." Rachel reached into her purse and pulled out the phone.

Gladys's eyes narrowed again. Apparently, the

older woman's dislike of technology extended far beyond her clock radio.

"I hate it when those ring during the service," Gladys said pointedly. "It's extremely rude."

"I agree." Rachel wondered sheepishly if Gladys was remembering the time Rachel had forgotten to turn hers off and had gotten a call during Tony's sermon. "That's why on Sunday mornings I don't even turn mine on."

Rachel hit the Power-On button and tinny classical music filled the air.

"It's telling me I have a message," Rachel said in response to Gladys's puzzled look.

"I'll bet it's from Jay," Gladys said excitedly, "telling you why he's not here. Aren't you going to listen?"

The way the older woman was eyeing the phone, Rachel had the feeling Gladys would have snatched it out of her hands and checked the message herself if she'd known how to do it.

"I will," Rachel said. "Unfortunately I don't have time right now. I need to catch Dottie before she leaves."

Flashing Gladys a bright smile, Rachel took off through the crowd before the older woman could stop her. The last thing she wanted was to call Jay— or even listen to his message—with Gladys hovering nearby, listening to every word, ready to grill her the minute she hung up.

Rachel chatted with Dottie for a several minutes before heading for the privacy of her car. Once inside the small import, Rachel dialed her voice mail and breathed a sigh of relief at the sound of Jay's voice.

"Hey, babe, it's me. Listen, I'm not going to be in church today. Last night when I got home there was a message on the machine. They fired my fill-in and Hugh wants me back on the air Monday morning. He's arranged for an early flight out of Des Moines. Dad and I are on our way to the airport now. I'll call you when I get to L.A. And, Rachel, I love you."

Her heart warmed briefly at his words before it hit her.

He's gone.

Rachel felt sick to her stomach, sick clear through to her soul. He'd captured her heart and now he was gone. And the worst of it was she had no idea when she'd see him again.

She immediately chided herself, reminding herself this was what she'd wanted. It was a blessing Jay had left when he did. After all, the longer he stayed, the harder it would have been to let him go.

If only she could get her aching heart to agree with that logic, she'd be set.

Chapter Nineteen

Rachel pulled into a space in front of the Grateful Bread Café and shoved the car into Park. Though the last thing she felt like doing was making small talk over pecan streusel coffee cake, she'd promised Dottie she'd stop by.

Heaving a resigned sigh, Rachel forced a smile to her face and grabbed her bag from the seat. But before she could open the door, the William Tell Overture started to play from deep inside her purse.

Her heart skipped a beat.

Jay.

She fumbled for the phone, finally pulling it free.

"Hello," she said, her voice sounding breathless.

"Good morning."

A surge of emotion so strong it brought tears to

her eyes rushed through Rachel at the sound of Jay's voice.

"It's not morning any longer," she said lightly, blinking rapidly. "It's already afternoon."

Jay laughed. "Well, it's still morning here in California and I'm ready for a nap."

"How early did you fly out?" Even as she asked, Rachel wondered why she was talking about such inconsequential things when there were so many more important things to discuss. She absently twisted the diamond on her finger.

"5:15," Jay said. "We left for the airport at 2:30."

It had been well after midnight when Jay had left her house so he couldn't have slept more than an hour or two. "I can see why you're tired."

"I'll survive the lack of sleep," Jay said. "But I'm not sure I'll survive not seeing you every day. I miss you already."

Rachel smiled into the phone and the tightness gripping her heart began to ease.

"I wish you were here," she said. "The old town isn't the same without you."

"I'll be back before you know it," he said.

It wouldn't be before she knew it—it would be Thanksgiving. And that was four months away. An eternity, no matter how you looked at it, and way too long to continue a silly charade.

Rachel's gaze dropped to her left hand, to the diamond she'd grown to love but now had to give up. "Jay, about the engagement—"

"Can I call you later?" he asked in a hurried tone. "I still need to get my luggage and grab a cab."

Rachel paused, not sure whether to be relieved or upset by the delay.

"Rachel?"

"I'm still here."

"Remember one thing."

Her fingers tightened around the receiver. "What's that?"

"I love you, babe. I really do."

Jay clicked off the phone and heaved a relieved sigh. She loved him. He could hear it in her voice. He still had a chance. It might not be a big one, but he'd take what he could get.

When he'd gotten the message from Hugh late last night, his first inclination had been to call Rachel. It was only natural. After all, for two months they'd shared everything. But last night she'd turned down his proposal and tried to give back his ring.

She'd been in the breakup mood. That's why instead of calling her, he'd packed his bags.

He didn't want her to make any hasty decisions. Above all, he wanted the ring to still be on her finger when he left town. The way he saw it, as long as she was wearing it, there was still a possibility she'd marry him and move to L.A.

But if she gave it back and told everyone in town they'd broken up, the chance of that happening was nonexistent.

No, the diamond needed to stay on her finger. Until he could convince her it should stay there for keeps.

"This is like old times." Lindsay snuggled close to Jay in the pew. "Why don't you come over to my place after the reception? We can catch up on old times."

The look in her eyes told Jay that the wedding of one of his co-workers to her longtime friend had put his former girlfriend in a romantic mood. It had been Jay's experience that these occasions brought out such emotions in women. That's why he'd come to the wedding stag.

But he hadn't been alone for long. He'd run into Lindsay in the parking lot and before he knew it, they were walking in and being seated together.

When he'd told her he was engaged, she'd just

laughed as if he'd said something funny and told
him how handsome he looked in Armani.

Lindsay was wearing a black silk halter dress
that reminded Jay more of a slip than a dress. But
she wore it well and judging from all the admiring
glances she was garnering, there were any number
of guys who would gladly take his place at her side.
But the only woman on Jay's mind tonight was
Rachel.

"I don't think my fiancée would approve." Jay
kept his tone deliberately light and softened his refusal with a smile.

"I've got a suggestion." Lindsay leaned close
and Jay caught a whiff of expensive perfume as a
perfectly manicured nail traveled up the front of
his shirt. "Don't tell farm girl. It can be our little
secret."

"She's not a farm girl." The minute the words left
his mouth Jay wondered why he'd even bothered.
Lindsay was firmly convinced everyone who lived
in Iowa farmed and nothing he said was going to
change her mind. "And Rachel and I don't keep secrets from each other."

"Oh, puh-leeze." Lindsay straightened in her seat
and brushed a tiny piece of lint from the front of her
bodice, her fingers lingering on the lace edging.

"Everyone has secrets. It's only natural. I'm sure Roxanne—"

"Rachel," Jay interjected.

"Whatever." Lindsay waved a dismissive hand. "Anyway, as I was saying, I'm sure your sweetie has secrets of her own."

Jay couldn't help but smile. If Lindsay had spent any time at all in a small town, she'd know there were no secrets there. And if she knew Rachel, she'd know that Rachel would never cheat. "Rachel isn't like that."

An ache of longing rose up inside him. He missed Rachel more every day. His life, which had once seemed so full, now felt empty and flat without her in it.

He still loved his job, but he loved Rachel, too.

What am I going to do if I lose her?

His palms grew damp. It had been three weeks since he'd left Millville. He called Rachel every day, but he could sense her pulling away.

Last night she'd asked him for suggestions on how they should "break up." Though he should have seen it coming, he hadn't known what to say. But he'd quickly improvised, telling her he had something in mind but was still firming up some of the details.

Thankfully, she'd let the subject drop. For now.

But it would come up again. Jay thought about what his father had told him: how God had helped him during the rough times in his marriage. Maybe the Almighty could help Jay, as well.

Dear God, I feel bad about shoving You to the back of my life and now coming to You with a request, but I desperately need a favor and I don't know where else to turn. I love Rachel and I know I can make her happy. I want to put You and my family before my career, but does that have to mean I have to give up doing what I love? Isn't there any way that both Rachel and I can have what we want? Please help me to find a way to make all of our dreams come true. Amen.

"…I don't know anyone else here," Lindsay said. "I wouldn't go at all but I've known the groom forever and I promised I'd make an appearance."

Jay looked up and realized that while he'd been lost in thought, Lindsay had continued to talk.

"Well?" she pressed when he remained silent.

He lifted a brow. "What was the question?"

Irritation skittered across the model's flawless face. "Will you go with me to the reception?"

Jay thought for a moment, then shrugged. After all, it wasn't like it was a date or anything. "Sure, I'll go."

* * *

Rachel swung by the bank after school on Monday. The drive-thru was packed so she parked out front and went inside, praying she wouldn't run into Tom. She hadn't seen him since that day at the church and she hadn't really missed him.

Thankfully, the lobby was empty and both tellers were open. It took less than a minute to complete the transaction. She smiled her thanks and took her cash.

"What a pleasant surprise."

Rachel stifled a groan at the familiar male voice. Plastering a smile on her lips, she turned. "Tom. Where have you been hiding out? I thought you'd dropped off the face of the earth."

"I've been out of town." He returned her polite smile with a friendly one of his own and she couldn't help but notice how fit and tanned he looked.

"Florida?" She vaguely remembered his family having a condo in Bonita Bay.

"Actually, the Caribbean," he said. "St. Barts."

Rachel nodded. "Well, you look great. I'd better be getting h—"

"Wait." Tom reached out a hand and stopped her hasty retreat. "Can you spare a few minutes? I've got something in my office to give you."

Rachel hesitated and glanced at her watch. "I don't have much time. My mother is coming over for dinner."

"It won't take long." Tom put his hand against the small of her back and urged her across the lobby. "I promise."

She'd been in his office many times. It sat toward the back of the bank past the open cubicles of his employees. Rachel felt their eyes on her, curious, no doubt, as to what she was doing there now that they were no longer a couple.

He let her enter first then pulled the door closed behind him. Rachel glanced around the room. "Where is it?"

"Where is what?"

"What you wanted to give me."

An uncomfortable look crossed Tom's face. "Actually I wanted to talk to you first."

Normally Tom was confident to the point of being arrogant, but today he appeared not only unsure but oddly vulnerable.

Rachel's heart softened. "What is it, Tom?"

He motioned for her to take a seat, but when she did, instead of sitting behind the desk, Tom remained standing. He rubbed his hands together and paced the small office. "I wanted to thank you for encouraging me to see a therapist. You were right. My behavior was something I needed to address. Dr. Peters thinks I'm making great progress."

"You're still seeing him?" Rachel couldn't keep the surprise from her voice. Though they hadn't discussed the issue since Tom had announced he'd met with the psychologist, she'd just assumed he had quit going after they'd broken up.

He nodded. "I'm also attending an anger management group. It was hard to admit I needed the help and I know if you hadn't pushed me, I'd never have done it."

The clock in Tom's office chimed and Rachel's eyes widened. She'd known she was running late, but not this late. She rose to her feet. "I'm happy for you, Tom. I really am."

He hesitated, measuring her for a moment. "There's one more thing."

"Something quick, I hope," Rachel said with a smile. "And good."

"I guess you could call it good," Tom said. "I mean, it's best to know the way things really are, rather than living in a fantasy world, right?"

Rachel's smile faded at the cryptic remark. She shifted uneasily from one foot to the other. "What are you talking about?"

Tom picked up a newspaper clipping from his desk and handed it to Rachel. "This pretty much says it all."

It was a picture and an accompanying article from the arts and entertainment section of the L.A. Times. Rachel immediately recognized Jay. A tightness gripped her chest at the sight of his pretty companion.

"I'm not sure who the woman is." Tom leaned over her shoulder. "The article says something about her being a model."

"Her name is Lindsay Stark." Rachel somehow managed to say the name with just the right amount of casual indifference. "She and Jay used to date."

"According to the article they're back together again," Tom said, his voice unusually soft and gentle.

Though Rachel told herself she was completely in control of her emotions, she found herself blinking back tears as she scanned the article. "Can I have this?"

"Sure." Tom's hand dropped to her shoulder. "I'm sorry I had to be the one to tell you, Rach, but I thought you'd want to know."

Want to know what? Rachel thought. That my fiancé is cheating on me? Even as the possibility flashed before her, Rachel rejected it. She knew Jay too well to believe he'd hooked up with his old girl-friend, no matter how attractive.

But why was he with her in the first place? It just didn't make sense.

I have something planned.

Jay's words came back to her in a rush. And with it, his earlier promise to take the heat for a breakup. The breath she didn't realize she'd been holding came out in a whoosh.

He'd staged the whole thing.

But why hadn't he told her what he'd done last night when they'd talked? Instead, he'd spent the whole time talking about some new church he was attending and how much he liked the minister. It didn't make sense. Unless he hadn't known for sure the story would get picked up by the wire services and hadn't wanted to get her hopes up.

Rachel stifled a sob at the irony. Any hope she once had was now gone.

It was over.

"If there's anything you need." Compassion filled Tom's voice. "Or if there's anything I can do for you, just ask. I care about you, Rachel. And, once I work through these issues, I still believe you and I could have a future together. I know we both want the same things out of life."

Rachel lifted her gaze to Tom. How could she tell him he had it all wrong? That the only thing she wanted out of life was the one thing she couldn't have.

"I need to go." She walked to the door and opened it.

"Remember what I said," Tom called after her as she slipped through the doorway and headed toward the lobby. "I'm here for you."

Rachel didn't look back. She kept her gaze focused straight ahead and walked with a brisk, determined gait through the lobby and out the front door. Crossing the sidewalk, she stepped off the curb and reached for her car door.

"Hey, little lady. What are you up to this afternoon?"

Rachel jumped at the unexpected greeting. She turned to see Henry Nordstrom standing on the edge of the sidewalk, a warm smile on his lips.

Rachel had always liked and respected Henry. If she and Jay had married, his father would have become hers. She knew in her heart that he'd have been the kind of dad you could depend on. The kind she'd never had; the kind she'd always wanted.

Rachel experienced a sudden urge to throw her arms around Henry and cry on his shoulder about the unfairness of life, but she was a grown woman, not a child, so instead she smiled in greeting and clasped her hands together to still their trembling. "Hello, Henry."

To her dismay, her voice broke slightly.

His eyes narrowed. He searched her face before his gaze dropped to the article she still held. "What's wrong?"

"Nothing," she said quickly, resisting the urge to shove the clipping into her bag. "Nothing at all."

"Let me see it." He held out a large weathered hand. Though his tone brooked no argument, the look in his eyes reflected his concern.

Rachel hesitated. The last thing she wanted was for him to be angry with Jay or think less of his son. Still, Jay had gone to a lot of work to set this up....

She stepped to the edge of the sidewalk and handed Henry the clipping. "It's about Jay and Lindsay."

Henry's gaze skimmed the article and his lips tightened. He stared at the picture for a long time, then handed it back to Rachel. "It doesn't mean anything."

"It doesn't?" Rachel couldn't keep the surprise from her voice.

"Of course not," Henry said. "My boy loves you. I know that. So do you."

"What about the picture?" Rachel asked. "And the article says—"

"Those newspaper people will write anything they think will sell papers," Henry said, with a dismissive wave. "This is simply a misunderstanding."

"A misunderstanding?" Rachel echoed.

"It's obvious the person who wrote that article doesn't know my son. Or you." Henry's chin lifted in a determined tilt. "Jay loves you. You love him. Tell me that isn't true."

The older man's loyalty brought the tears back to Rachel's eyes. "Sometimes love isn't enough. Sometimes it's just…impossible for a couple to go the distance."

"You'll make it work." Henry reached out and awkwardly patted Rachel's shoulder. "The pastor told me something once that helped my missus and me when we were going through hard times. He said that when things look the darkest, we needed to remember that we're not alone. God is on our side. And with God on our side, nothing is impossible."

Rachel opened her mouth to argue, then shut it without speaking. Regardless of what Henry said or believed, her engagement to Jay was over.

And regardless what her heart said, her head told her it was for the best.

Chapter Twenty

"More coffee, Mother?" Rachel pushed aside a half-eaten piece of Dutch apple pie and held up the silver carafe.

"Only if you'll join me," Shirley Tanner said with a smile.

"Of course I will," Rachel said.

She filled her mother's cup as well as her own before resuming her seat at the kitchen table.

"That was a wonderful dinner." Shirley Tanner stabbed a slice of apple with her fork. "And dessert is fabulous, as always. But—"

Rachel stilled, the rim of the china cup pressed against her lips. She lowered the cup to the saucer when her mother didn't continue. "But?"

Shirley leaned forward, her eyes filled with concern. "You've not been yourself tonight. Oh, you've put on a good show but I can tell something is wrong. Did you and Jay have a fight?"

The tears that Rachel had held back all evening slipped down her cheeks. This was the perfect opportunity to tell her mother the engagement was over, but the words wouldn't come.

"Oh, honey," her mother said softly, reaching across the table to take Rachel's hand. "You two will work it out."

"I don't think so." Rachel took a deep breath and swiped at her tears with a napkin.

Her mother sighed. "Tell me what's going on."

Rachel paused. Her mother had been Rachel's best friend for as long as she could remember and she wanted to be honest with her.

"I love Jay," Rachel said. "But I'm smart enough to realize that a marriage between us would never work."

"Because of that newspaper article?"

Rachel glanced up in surprise. "How do you know about that?"

Her mother's cheeks pinked. "You ran into Henry this afternoon."

Rachel nodded. "At the bank."

"Well, he called Twyla," her mother's voice quickened. "She called me."

"And?" Rachel found herself being more curious than angry.

"Do you really believe Jay is cheating on you?"

"No, of course not," Rachel said quickly.

"Then I'm confused," Shirley said. "Why do you think a marriage between you and Jay won't work?"

"It's a lot of things. It's his job. It's where he needs to live to further his career." Rachel started to add "it's his lack of faith," but she was no longer sure that was a valid point. Jay's faith might be a work-in-progress, but she could tell by their phone conversations that he was on the right track. "The last thing I want is the kind of home life I had growing up for my children."

Surprise skittered across her mother's face. "What do you mean?"

"Dad worked long hours at the store," Rachel said bluntly. "He was never around. You never did anything together as a couple. We never did anything together as a family. Everything came second to the store."

"The place kept him busy." Her mother's eyes took on a distant faraway look. "But it was also his excuse. Our home life had more to do with the kind of man your father was inside rather than his job.

Even if he'd have had all the time in the world, it wouldn't have made a difference."

"Still—"

"Still, nothing," Shirley said. "Marriage is about caring. It's about compromise. And it's about sacrifice."

"I've told you," Rachel said, wondering how her mother could have missed such an important point. "Jay isn't willing to—"

"Forget about Jay for a moment," her mother said. "Let's talk about Rachel Ann. What sacrifice is she willing to make?"

Rachel shifted uncomfortably in her seat.

"I like it here," Rachel said finally. "You're here. All my friends are here. In L.A., I'd be surrounded by strangers."

"My mother once told me that strangers are just friends we haven't yet met," her mother said with a smile. "But it's your choice, honey. I just want you to think this through."

"He won't live here." Rachel lifted her chin. "Not even for me."

"And you won't live in L.A.," her mother said calmly. "Not even for him."

Rachel sighed. "We're at an impasse."

"You're at a crossroads." Shirley leaned back in

her chair and studied her daughter for a long moment. "And the answer to one simple question will chart your course for years to come."

Rachel lifted a brow. "What question is that?"

Her mother met Rachel's gaze. "How far are you willing to go for the sake of love?"

"You're leaving?" Jay couldn't keep the surprise from his voice. When Kathi had suggested lunch at a trendy café near the studio, he'd thought she'd wanted to discuss the most recent ratings. Instead she'd told him she'd found another job.

Kathi smiled and sipped her chai. "October fifteen is my last day. Rick is already in Lincoln looking for a place to live."

"I can't believe you're moving to Nebraska." Jay had friends in Lincoln and while it was a nice college town, it was small, with barely a quarter of a million residents.

"It all happened so fast, sometimes it's hard for me to believe it, too," Kathi said. "The evening anchor who'd been in that spot for a bazallion years left and a friend happened to mention the opening. I had my agent check it out and, voilà, I had a new job."

Jay knew it was probably not as easy as all that,

but snagging a woman with Kathi's experience had to be a great coup for the station.

"But why Nebraska?" Jay asked.

"Like you, Rick and I have a lot of family in that part of the country," she said. "It'll be nice to be close to them. Especially as Tyler gets older."

"But your career—"

"Isn't as important to me as it once was." A wry grin twisted Kathi's lips. "There, I've said it. I bet you never thought you'd hear those words coming from my mouth."

She was right. Like him, Kathi had started at a small station straight out of college and had willingly moved every time a better opportunity came along.

"What made you decide to take such a drastic step?" For the past few weeks, Jay had been struggling with what to do about his own career.

On one hand he missed Rachel so much, he couldn't imagine spending one more day without her. On the other hand, he couldn't imagine spending the rest of his life at some small station in Iowa reporting hog futures.

"You know as well as I do that there's a lot of pressure in this job. While you were gone it started affecting my home life." Kathi's gaze dropped to her plate. "I began taking out my frustrations on the ones I loved most."

"Did Rick give you an ultimatum?" Jay asked, knowing it was none of his business but still curious.

"He didn't have to," Kathi said, meeting his gaze. "I love this job, but I love my family more."

"So you sacrificed your career for them."

"It's not a sacrifice." Kathi leaned forward, resting her elbows on the table. "It's a choice I'm making and quite willingly. Not because I *have* to, but because I *want* to."

"I don't understand."

"I want it all, Jay," Kathi said. "I want to be in front of the cameras and do the work I love *and* have a home life. I can have that in Lincoln. I no longer believe I can have that here."

"But you were rumored to be the frontrunner for that slot that will be opening up at—"

"Life is about choices," Kathi interrupted. "It's about priorities. Success is meaningless without someone you love by your side."

Jay thought about Rachel. Any success he achieved wouldn't be nearly as sweet without her by his side. Could he do it? Could he willingly give up everything he'd worked for all these years for the sake of love?

* * *

The door to Jay's office opened but he didn't bother looking up from the computer screen.

"Jackie, were you able to book me on that flight to Des Moines?" Jay asked his gaze still focused on the screen.

"I'm not Jackie." Though the hesitant voice was decidedly feminine, it didn't belong to his assistant. "But I do know a thing or two about Des Moines."

Jay's head jerked up and for a moment he just stared, certain he had to be hallucinating. Because standing in the doorway, looking every inch a California girl with her blond hair, blue eyes and lithe figure was the one woman he'd never expected to see in L.A.

Jay blinked, convinced his longing for Rachel had conjured her up.

She didn't disappear.

He blinked again.

Her smile faded and two lines of worry appeared between her brows. "I wasn't sure if you'd be happy to see me or if—"

Jay wasted no time in showing her just how much he'd missed her. Quickly covering the distance between them, he tugged her toward him, reaching with his right hand to pull her chin up and stopping her words by covering her mouth with his own.

He kissed her with all the love and longing that had been pent up inside him the past month, and when it ended he kept his arms around her, breathing in the clean fresh scent that was Rachel.

"I can't believe you're here." Jay sighed into her hair, perfectly and utterly content.

But Rachel stepped back, resisting his efforts to pull her to him once again. She squared her shoulders. "I'm here because there's a decision I have to make and to do that I need some answers."

His heart stilled at the serious look in her eye, but Jay forced a smile. "Ask me anything, anything at all."

"That thing with Lindsay," Rachel said. "What was that about?"

Jay's brows pulled together. "What thing with Lindsay?"

Rachel stared at him for a long moment then reached inside her purse. "This."

The minute Jay saw the newspaper article and picture he groaned. "I can't believe you saw that."

The reporter who'd done the piece hadn't bothered to interview him and Jay wasn't sure who'd snapped the photo. The article was tabloid fodder, pure and simple. The thought that Rachel might see it and be concerned hadn't occurred to him.

But somehow she had, and it had upset her. Jay cursed the irresponsible journalism that had caused this unnecessary pain.

"Is it true?"

"Some of it," Jay said, determined to be honest. "I did run into Lindsay at a wedding and we did attend the reception together."

Rachel stared unblinkingly. "Are you two back together?"

"No way." Jay laughed out loud at the thought. Being around Lindsay those few hours had made him only miss Rachel more.

"But the article—"

"Got it all wrong," Jay said firmly.

"I thought you might have staged the whole thing," Rachel said in a remarkably calm voice, twisting a strand of hair between her fingers.

"Why would I do that?"

Rachel lifted one shoulder in a slight shrug. "Maybe because you think it's time our engagement comes to an end?"

Jay met her gaze. "What I think, Miss Tanner, is that it's time you and I have a heart-to-heart."

Chapter Twenty-One

Rachel's breath caught in her throat at the determined look in his eye. A cold chill raced up her spine.

"I'd like to speak first," Rachel said quickly. "If you don't mind."

Jay opened his mouth as if to protest, but appeared to reconsider and shut it without uttering a word. He gestured to a leather sofa against the wall. "Shall we sit?"

"That'd be nice." Though Rachel walked with a confident stride, her insides were trembling.

She took a seat on the sofa and Jay settled in beside her.

Rachel swallowed hard and wondered if she'd made a mistake. Maybe she should have let him go first. What if she bared her soul and he rejected her?

After all, he was back in his element now—a handsome, successful man surrounded by beautiful women. Maybe he'd only thought he was in love with her and had now realized his error.

The urge to flee with pride intact was almost overwhelming. Rachel started to push up from the sofa, but before she could even shift positions, Jay reached over and took her hand in his.

"I hope you don't mind," he said. "But I can't be so close to you and not touch you. It's just not possible."

The warmth from his hand traveled up her arm and straight to her heart, renewing her flagging hope. She took a deep breath and plunged ahead before she lost her nerve.

"I've been doing a lot of thinking since you left," Rachel said. "Not just about you, but about me, about my life and what it is I really want."

Though Jay didn't move a muscle, Rachel could feel him tense.

"And what did you discover?" he asked.

"That making God a priority in my life was still the right decision," she said. "That family and friends were important."

His hand tightened around hers but he didn't say a word.

"But I also realized that I'd been wrong about some things, too," she said. "I'd been so happy in Millville that I confused a place, a location on the map, with what home really is."

He stared, unblinking. "You've lost me."

"Home is where the heart is," Rachel said. "It's not a town, or a house, or a building. It's being with the one you love."

"What are you saying?"

"That I love you," she said. "And home for me will be wherever you are. If that's here in Los Angeles, then so be it. So, if you still want to marry me, I'm here to say yes."

Hope filled Jay's eyes but his expression remained cautious. "You'll be giving up so much."

"I don't look at it that way anymore," Rachel said.

"Are you sure?" Thick emotion filled Jay's voice.

Rachel gave one last thought to her friends and family back in Millville. She smiled. "Positive."

Suddenly she found herself in his arms, his lips covering her face with kisses and she was laughing and kissing him back.

"You *have* missed me," she said teasingly as his lips traveled down her neck.

"You have no idea," he said, lifting his head. "Every day was pure torture."

"Well, the torture has officially ended," she said. "Now all that's left is for me to officially resign and for us to set a wedding date."

"Can you get out of your contract?" he asked.

"Not a problem," Rachel said. "My aunt is on the school board. She said if I got a better offer in L.A., I should go for it."

Rachel leaned forward and nibbled at his ear. "I think I've got a much better offer."

Jay groaned but instead of kissing her as she'd hoped, he straightened and sat back. "You told me once you didn't want to live in L.A."

"I *want* to be where you are," she said.

He studied her for a long moment, his gaze sharp and assessing.

"I've been thinking it might be nice to move somewhere closer to home," he said finally. "Maybe Kansas City or Denver? Or even Chicago?"

Rachel's brows drew together. Now she was thoroughly confused. "But you have a good job here."

"I do," he said. "But it's a long ways from home."

"It never bothered you to be so far away before," Rachel pointed out.

He leaned in close and whispered in her ear. "I've never had a wife before."

"You'd do this for me?" She couldn't keep the surprise from her voice.

"I'd do it for us." The look he shot her was filled with pure love. "For you, for me, for the children we'll one day have. And, if you don't like any of those cities, we'll downsize again if necessary, until we find the perfect fit."

Rachel snuggled up against him. "I've already found the perfect fit."

Jay's arms tightened around her. "I promise I'll do everything in my power to make you happy."

Rachel laid her head against his chest, utterly content. She breathed in the scent of him, reveling in the words of love he murmured, in the touch of his hand against her hair.

If home was indeed where the heart is, Rachel knew that in this skyscraper overlooking the City of Angels, nestled in the arms of the man she loved, she'd found her home.

Epilogue

Two Years Later

"You have to know that what you're doing is dangerous," Dottie said with mock seriousness. "Moving so close to Millville almost guarantees you'll have a steady stream of visitors. And once that baby arrives in a couple of months, that stream will turn into a raging river."

"I want you all to drop by," Rachel said, glancing around the table. "The more often, the better."

Although it had been after midnight when she and Jay had arrived in Millville, word had quickly spread and Dottie had arranged an impromptu luncheon at her house. In addition to Rachel and Jay,

Tony and Claire and Adam and Jocelyn had been invited.

As usual, after eating, the men had disappeared into the living room while the women remained in the kitchen.

"The house we bought has an extra bedroom specifically for guests," Rachel added.

"John and I always go to Kansas City to check out the Christmas lights," Dottie said. "Put us down for mid-December."

"I'm not waiting that long," Claire said. "I desperately need some new clothes. Just let me know when you're settled and Tony and I will be on your doorstep. I love to shop at the Plaza."

"I've got an idea," Jocelyn said. "What would all of you think about making plans to get together on a regular basis—say every other month? Rachel and Jay could come up here or we could all go down there?"

Happiness spread through Rachel like warm molasses. "Sounds good to me."

"I'm all for it," Claire said.

"It's a great idea." Dottie smiled. "I'm afraid if we didn't have plans, we wouldn't see you up here as much as we'd like. Especially now that your mother is in Kansas City."

Shirley Tanner had always hated living so far away from her oldest daughter and her grandchildren. That's why, when Rachel had announced that not only had Jay taken a job in Kansas City, but that they were pregnant, her mother had put her house on the market.

Once it had sold, she'd bought a house in Overland Park, fifteen minutes from Rachel and Jay's new home and thirty minutes from Mary.

"Are you kidding? I'd still come and see you guys," Rachel said. "But this way, we know we'll get together regularly."

"I bet you can't wait to get out of Los Angeles," Dottie said, visibly shuddering. "All that horrible traffic and smog."

Rachel smiled. That had been her first impression of the city, too, but she'd quickly discovered all L.A. had to offer and had grown to love it.

"Actually, I'm going to miss California," Rachel said, thinking of all the new friends she'd made. "I really liked the school where I taught and I absolutely loved the warm winters."

"Whose decision was it to make the move to K.C.?" Jocelyn asked.

"Jay had offered to move closer even before we were married. But he was doing so well, I convinced him that I wanted to give L.A. a chance," Rachel said. "Then, four months ago when I found out I was pregnant, Jay brought it up again."

"And this time you said yes," Dottie said.

"Actually, at first I said no, but when Jay convinced me that he really wanted to raise his children in the Midwest," Rachel said an impish smile, "I told him I'd make the big sacrifice and move back."

The words had barely left her mouth when the men piled into the kitchen, declaring they were in desperate need of snack food. Dottie and Jocelyn laughed, telling the men they'd just eaten even as they rose to assist John and Adam in their foraging. When Claire announced she'd check on the napping children upstairs, Tony promptly volunteered to go with her.

The last one to enter the kitchen was Jay. Rachel caught sight of him just as he stepped through the doorway.

Their eyes met and her heart flip-flopped. It was incredible. Even after two years of marriage, one look from Jay was still all it took to steal her breath away. She couldn't begin to imagine life without him. He brought a richness and a depth to her world that went far beyond the physical.

He moved to her side and crouched down, brushing a kiss against her cheek even as his hand moved to rest on her protruding belly.

"How's my girl?" he asked.

"She's fine." Rachel smiled. "Active as ever. A few minutes ago she kicked so hard it knocked the napkin off my lap."

Jay chuckled. "I'm glad for the baby update, but actually I was asking about *you*. Don't forget, you're my girl, too. My best girl."

Rachel leaned her head against his shoulder.

"I love you," she said in a low voice meant for his ears only. "Forever."

"For always," he whispered.

As his lips met hers and the baby kicked inside her, Rachel realized that her mother had been right; a sacrifice made for the sake of love wasn't a sacrifice at all.

* * * * *

Dear Reader,

Often when I write a book, the secondary characters become so vivid in my mind that I know they simply have to have a book of their own. However, when I wrote *Redeeming Claire* (Love Inspired, October 2001) Jay and Rachel must have been below my radar. It was not until a reader, Carolyn Jean Brown, wrote to me and suggested a love match between the two that I stared to see the possibilities. *For Love's Sake* is the result.

I hope you enjoy their story.

Blessings,

Cynthia Rutledge

Love Inspired®

LOVE CAME UNEXPECTEDLY

BY

RUTH SCOFIELD

Inheriting a fishing resort from her grandfather wasn't something Sunny Merrill had ever expected—she'd been orphaned at a young age and hadn't ever met the man. Always there to lend a hand was neighbor Grant Prentiss, the handsome rancher and riding stable owner who knew a lot about Sunshine Acres. Yet their unexpected love was threatened by a secret Grant was keeping from her....

Don't miss

LOVE CAME UNEXPECTEDLY

On sale January 2005

Available at your favorite retail outlet.

Love Inspired®

TO HEAL A HEART

BY

ARLENE JAMES

Finding a handwritten letter at the airport offering
forgiveness to an unknown recipient put widowed
lawyer Mitch Sayer on a quest to uncover its
addressee…until he sat down next to Piper Wynne.
His lovely seatmate made him temporarily forget his
mission. After the flight, he kept running into Piper,
whose eyes hid painful secrets…including the fact
that the letter was written to her!

Don't miss

TO HEAL A HEART
On sale January 2005

Available at your favorite retail outlet.

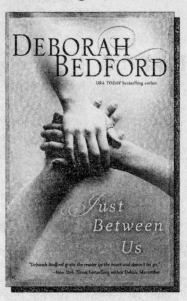

Take 2 inspirational love stories FREE!

PLUS get a FREE surprise gift!

Mail to Steeple Hill Reader Service™

In U.S.
3010 Walden Ave.
P.O. Box 1867
Buffalo, NY 14240-1867

In Canada
P.O. Box 609
Fort Erie, Ontario
L2A 5X3

YES! Please send me 2 free Love Inspired® novels and my free surprise gift. After receiving them, if I don't wish to receive anymore, I can return the shipping statement marked cancel. If I don't cancel, I will receive 4 brand-new novels every month, before they're available in stores! Bill me at the low price of $4.24 each in the U.S. and $4.74 each in Canada, plus 25¢ shipping and handling and applicable sales tax, if any*. That's the complete price and a savings of over 10% off the cover prices—quite a bargain! I understand that accepting the books and gift places me under no obligation ever to buy any books. I can always return a shipment and cancel at any time. Even if I never buy another book from Steeple Hill, the 2 free books and the surprise gift are mine to keep forever.

113 IDN DZ9M
313 IDN DZ9N

Name	(PLEASE PRINT)	

Address	Apt. No.	

City	State/Prov.	Zip/Postal Code

Not valid to current Love Inspired® subscribers.

Want to try two free books from another series?
Call 1-800-873-8635 or visit www.morefreebooks.com.

* Terms and prices are subject to change without notice. Sales tax applicable in New York. Canadian residents will be charged applicable provincial taxes and GST. All orders subject to approval. Offer limited to one per household.

® are registered trademarks owned and used by the trademark owner and or its licensee.

INTLI04R   ©2004 Steeple Hill